THE TORMENTED

THE SISTER VERONICA MYSTERIES #BOOK 3

SARAH SHERIDAN

www.bloodhoundbooks.com

Print ISBN 978-1-914614-45-3

ALSO BY SARAH SHERIDAN

For Rich, thank you for being so amazing.

1

Exactly two hours before the first murder occurred, Sister Veronica piled a lump of slow-roasted lamb on to her fork whilst staring intently at the teenage girl opposite her. She was wondering, for the tenth time that day, why on earth she'd accepted her cousin Florence's invitation to spend Christmas at Chalfield Hall. Fantasies of peacefully reuniting with family she hadn't seen for nearly forty years had evaporated shortly after her arrival the previous day – a cruel reality check mainly brought on by Florence's granddaughter's behaviour. It was almost impressive that Coco Beresford managed to bring any conversation or event round to herself in seconds, Sister Veronica reflected, with each encounter ending in hysteria and recriminations unless the adult being targeted – usually her father Magnus – immediately capitulated to her demands.

'I want a new car, Daddy,' Coco was whining over her barely touched food. 'It's not fair. Papa is always buying new cars, and I really need another one. Please, Daddy, can you get me one after Christmas? Promise me you will?'

Papa, Coco's grandfather Giles Beresford, smiled indulgently at her from the end of the table as his jowly chops moved with grinding intensity. It was true, he had just been regaling his guests with tales of his latest acquisition's engine size, Sister Veronica agreed, watching him run a hand through hair that had once been bright red but was now a blondish silver. And it had been a very dreary monologue, full of self-congratulatory pride.

'Good girl,' Giles said, spraying half-chewed meat morsels around. Several became lodged in his drooping handlebar moustache. 'That's the spirit. If you don't ask you don't get. Pound your father down until he agrees.' He winked at his granddaughter over the remnants of the feast.

Each of the fifteen extended family members – most in various states of insobriety around the table – had been presented with a plate of steaming roast lamb and spiced berry sauce by Florence as they entered the room. Encouraged to sit down and help themselves to an array of vegetables, different types of potato dishes and vats of home-made gravy, most of the serving plates down the centre of the table were now empty, except the bowl containing sprouts. Sister Veronica hadn't eaten so well – or so much – for years. The food, Florence told her, had been prepared earlier by Mrs Hardman, the part-time house-keeper and general home help who she had yet to meet. This woman seemed to flit in and out like an invisible spirit, whip-ping up culinary delights, then leaving them in the oven for the family to reheat at their leisure. She must thank her when they finally did meet, she reflected, for her superb fare. It was much more enjoyable than most of the conversations going on around her.

She sent Giles a sideways glance, her eyebrow raised, whisking a stray strand of grey hair from her eyes. She'd always found his greedy attitude towards possessions and life in general somewhat stomach-turning. He always wanted more; more money, more status, more prestige. Why not just enjoy what you've got, she'd wondered more than once. Instead of bull-dozing on through life and never being grateful for its rewards?

'We'll see,' Magnus grunted, not meeting his daughter's gaze. He was a bloated, tired man with fading strawberry-blond hair, the only child of Florence and Giles. His personality appeared to have been sucked out and exterminated by his ex-wife Romilly, if the others' accounts were to be believed. Sister Veronica had never met the woman but was intrigued by the sound of her, and rather wanted to meet and assess the person allegedly responsible for Magnus' character annihilation. From the brief comments she'd picked up from her cousin and Giles, Romilly sounded like a she-devil crossed with a piranha-eating parasite, blessed with the superhuman power of being able to destroy another human being through her words. Sister Veronica watched Magnus turn away from his daughter's protruding eyes and trembling mouth. *Probably wants to avoid a scene at the dinner table*, she thought to herself. *Good luck with that one, old fellow.* From what she'd seen so far, Coco seemed to relish an audience and wasn't one to put on a show of good manners just because guests were present.

'You only need a new car because you crashed the Nissan,' Wilfred said, turning to his sister as he laid his cutlery neatly on top of his empty plate. He pushed his glasses further up his nose and shook the mop of brown hair out of his eyes. 'If Daddy buys you another one, you might crash that one too. And that would be a waste of money, wouldn't it?' Ah, good old Wilfred. Sister Veronica supressed a smile. Just fifteen years old and already the most sensible in his family. His way of dealing with his demanding older sibling was to frequently take the wind out of her sails with a well-aimed remark. And who could blame him? Sister Veronica already had a headache after spending twenty-four hours with the girl and her other irritating relatives and was considering coming up with a fantastic excuse to get herself away from Northamptonshire and back to London. Perhaps she could say that Mother Superior had become poorly and was demanding that she return to the Convent of the Christian Heart at once? But then again, maybe it would be better not to tempt fate. If she did say such a thing, and then Mother Superior really became ill, the guilt would be too much to bear and she'd had enough of that over the last year, what with one thing and another.

'Oh SHUT UP, Wilfred,' Coco screamed, her eyes immediately wet with tears. 'Oh my *God*, why do you always have to bring that up? I was really hurt in that accident, wasn't I, Granny?' She turned to Florence, who was slumped at the other end of the table. 'Tell Wilfred to leave me alone. Tell him about my whiplash again. GRANNY! Why don't you ever listen to me? Granny! Look at me! Tell Wilfred not to bring the crash up EVER again.'

Florence looked up.

'Sorry, dear?' she said. *Her face is so white,* Sister Veronica thought. *And her eyes are so unfocused. She's hasn't been listening to anything anyone's said for at least five minutes. And she's only been drinking water, doesn't seem to drink alcohol much, so what on earth is wrong? Something's troubling her. But why hasn't she told me what it is?*

It was because of her cousin Florence that Sister Veronica knew she wouldn't really go through with her fantasies of escaping the dysfunction at Chalfield Hall, however much she might feel the urge. She couldn't help feeling something was wrong there, and that Florence had asked her to come for a particular purpose. Although what that was, she hadn't yet said, despite her subtle attempts at probing over the last twenty-four hours.

Since her arrival the day before, Sister Veronica had become increasingly concerned about Flo, as she called her. It had been unexpected enough to receive an invitation – quite out of the blue – asking her to spend Christmas at the old Gothic pile she used to visit infrequently as a child. While she and Flo had played together when they were young during family meetups, memorably commandeered by mad old Henrietta – Florence's mother – they'd drifted apart in their late teens. Sister Veronica, of course, had taken her vows and committed her life to God, entering the Convent of the Christian Heart in her early twenties, and Florence had managed to fall in love with the dullest man on earth, Giles Beresford; marrying him soon after and promising her life to him. She'd stuck unerringly to this pledge ever since, as far as Sister Veronica could see, and seemed to have endless patience, or perhaps blind denial, patiently putting up with his self-righteous outbursts and self-interested stories.

Before her arrival, Sister Veronica had been hoping that the years would have mellowed Giles, making his personality more palatable and less tedious. After all, she hadn't seen the man for nearly fifty years, and was prepared to start relations with him anew, giving him the benefit of the doubt. But during her brief time there she'd already found that – if anything – he was worse; more bullish, conceited and self-righteous than ever, and she found herself wanting to exit any room he was holding court in. It seemed that the feeling was mutual, and that Giles wished she'd never come to stay. While his greeting had been courteous when he'd picked her up from Towcester train station, his eyes had been cold, and they'd spent the journey to Little Ashby in silence, with Sister Veronica wishing it had been Florence who'd arrived to be her chauffeur. Giles had politely ignored her since, subtly enough so that only she would notice, still externally playing the good host for everyone else's purpose, but in reality never meeting her eye or paying her any true attention. She couldn't help wondering why this was, whether her natural dislike of him had shown through her usually good manners, or if there was another reason she was not yet aware of. Perhaps there was something he didn't want her to know about, or see? *No, stop it, Veronica, for goodness' sake*, she thought immediately. *Just for once, you are going to have a normal family week, with no dramatic traumas – not including Coco's behaviour – or mysteries occurring, so stop seeing problems where there are none. There doesn't have to be an unexpected puzzle to solve everywhere you go, so just relax for heaven's sake.*

But, she instantly argued with herself, what if there *were* problems at Chalfield that required her attention? Her sense of suspicion was particularly heightened due to the fact that she'd hardly slept a wink the night before. This was – in large part – due to the sense of unease that had clouded over her as soon as she'd stepped foot inside the house. Given that she didn't generally hold with any sixth sense clairvoyant type of thinking, she was finding this unsettling feeling of doom very irritating. But try as she might to shake it off, she couldn't help but keep going back to the notion that something bad might be afoot there. It was a bodily sensation that was bothering her, a feeling of warning in her blood, a shivery sense of forthcoming gloom in her mind. She hadn't quite got over the time, several months previously, when a woman had insisted on reading her tarot cards and had predicted destruction and fire, only for this to – at least in part – come true a few hours later. Sister Veronica still held the view that the whole thing was a load of rot, believing the tarot reading and the awful events that had followed it were nothing more than an unfortunate coincidence. Which made her current sense of impending tragedy even more frustrating and confusing. Perhaps it was all the rich food she'd eaten lately? She shook her head a little, willing the perception to go away.

To Giles' right, sat Maud, his plump, pink-faced aging cousin, who was very nice and polite to everyone in a benign and non-committal way. She didn't offer many opinions of her own during conversations, instead seeming happy to grin at whoever was talking and laugh when other people did. She tended to carry a cluster of knitting around – usually the wool was pink – but she seemed to have parted with this for the purpose of dinner. Sister Veronica did not mind Maud, in the same way that she didn't object to a vase of flowers or an old cat who curled up in the corner asleep. But she'd never been able to get to know the woman properly, largely because Maud offered no discernible personality to get to grips with, so had come to the conclusion that it was best to regard her as part of the furnishings.

On top of the ordeal of being unwillingly reunited with Giles, and trying to ignore the strange sense that something was wrong at the house, Sister Veronica hadn't realised such a large collection of extended family was also going to be present for Christmas. Sly old Florence hadn't told her that little detail, probably knowing the invitation would have been politely declined if the quantity of intended relatives *had* been disclosed. Which made the situation even more perplexing; her cousin obviously wanted her there, and had gone to some length to procure her company, but since she'd arrived had been tight-lipped about whatever reason might be behind the solicitation, despite looking frankly ill with stress.

Perhaps she was just run down, Sister Veronica mused, as she reached over to pour Flo some water, noticing that her cousin's usually well-maintained, dyed-blonde hair was showing at least two inches of grey roots. If she was honest, the present company was enough to cause anyone anxiety. She herself would have to take a painkiller if she sat there much longer; the throbbing in her head was intensifying. She watched as tall, skinny Coco stood up, cuffed her brother round the head and flounced out of the room, shaking her chestnut curls dramatically behind her before giving the dining-room door a hefty slam. The girl exited most rooms in much the same manner, she'd noticed.

Coco, her brother Wilfred and father Magnus had apparently moved back in with Florence and Giles after Magnus' marriage breakdown, Florence had confided quietly to her the previous evening. Before that they'd been living in a cottage in the village, Little Ashby, that lay nestled in a valley down the road from Chalfield Hall. The children's mother Romilly was still always in and out, which was a disturbing influence on everyone as she and Magnus tended to end up arguing, but Magnus never seemed to be able to have the power to stop his ex-wife from intruding. She was another woman Sister Veronica had yet to meet.

Magnus didn't seem to be able – or inclined – to parent his needy daughter, while Wilfred appeared to be almost entirely self-sufficient. Moreover, Magnus' family's return to Chalfield Hall didn't sit very well with Florence's brother Barnaby and his wife Cecily – who had also been invited to the old house for the festive season – and Sister Veronica thought Cecily's muttered, bitter remarks at lunch yesterday seemed to point to the fact that they were hoping they'd have a turn of living at Chalfield themselves in the not-too-distant future, with Magnus' return rather hampering their plans. Perhaps they'd been hoping Florence and Giles would quietly move out into a retirement bungalow or something. No chance there, she reflected. Giles would never give up living in the biggest house of all the relatives, you'd have to kill him first.

She glanced over at Barnaby and Cecily, a couple who must both be in their late sixties if she was correct. Barnaby, a formerly very successful lawyer by all accounts, was doing what he seemed to do best, which was staring vacantly into space, his white hair and moustache as unkempt as usual, his mind obviously away into another realm that was as far from the dining room as possible. Cecily, who'd technically been a homemaker but had put the children in nursery full time as soon as they were weaned, was leaning over to him, whispering something behind her hand, her thin face tight, her eyes narrowed. She'd been beautiful once, Sister Veronica remembered. But unfortunately her bitter personality had become increasingly etched on her features as she'd aged. She was probably muttering a petty malicious comment to her husband; she could remember the woman behaving in a similar way last time they'd met, all those years ago, when she'd been nice to people's faces but vitriolic behind their backs. Such a shame to have such a person in the party, it always made for bad feeling. People's defence mechanisms started kicking in, as they wondered what was being whispered about them behind closed doors. Sister Veronica could clearly recall what she'd heard Cecily say the day before about Florence and Giles being selfish house-hoggers who never looked after any of the extended family, only having eyes for their wastrel of a son. That they should have moved out years ago, and clearly couldn't handle such a big house, especially given the state of the garden. Barnaby didn't show any sign of listening to a word his wife was saying.

To make matters more chaotic, Barnaby and Cecily's two daughters Araminta and Lucinda – now known as Lucie – had also turned up, Araminta complete with husband Rufus. The girls had been spoiled with material gifts as children, Florence had told her in letters over the years, always wearing the most expensive clothes, but sadly never really being given proper attention by their parents who'd treated their arrival in the world as an inconvenience, an irritating dampening of their social life. Perhaps as a result of this, Araminta and Lucie had developed into two types of extremes, clinging on desperately to what gave meaning to their lives; the former, Araminta, marrying a man with money and living an utterly indulged and pampered lifestyle while apparently not truly caring much about anything. And the latter – Lucie – turning her back on such ways and transforming into a hard-working socialist, marrying – out of love – a man with no money. She seemed to care rather a lot about the awful problems in the world, to the point where it almost made her ill.

Sister Veronica looked over at Araminta and Rufus. They were already on their third bottle of wine, opulent in their expensive clothes, their cheeks magenta, and their unchecked criticism in full flow. They were currently laughing at Coco's dramatic departure.

'It's your fault for having children, old chap,' Rufus was saying to Magnus as he reached for a new bottle. 'I have no sympathy for you whatsoever. And to think, you could have been sensible and chosen a brat-free life like Minty and I. We can travel whenever we want, spend our money just how we please, and I'm planning to retire next year at the grand old age of forty-eight because I don't have to work my fingers to the bone trying to save an inheritance for any blood-sucking offspring.'

'Yes,' Araminta said, nodding enthusiastically. 'Exactly, Rufie. I personally can't stand teenagers, they're all so bloody moody. If we did have one they'd be packed off to boarding school until they were at least eighteen.'

'Yup.' Rufus gave a loud chuckle. 'Then I'd go and collect them from the gates, shake their hand, say well done, and send them out into the world to make a living. There's too much molly-coddling of children that goes on these days if you ask me. Doesn't do them any favours. Stops them from becoming independent and actually getting off their arses to achieve anything.'

Magnus just stared at his glass of wine, saying nothing, his shoulders drooping.

'*I'm* not bloody moody,' Wilfred called down the table,

shaking his hair from his eyes. *Good Lord*, Sister Veronica thought, looking at his untamed mop, *that boy needs a haircut with urgency.* 'And I've achieved quite a lot, I've taken four GCSEs a year early and I got top marks in all of them.' But Araminta and Rufus were concentrating on refilling their glasses and took no notice of him. Sister Veronica gave Wilfred an encouraging smile. She'd rather warmed to the fact-loving, serious boy, and couldn't help silently agreeing with his prosaic assessments of his seventeen-year-old sister. But she must be careful not to laugh or smile at him if his comments became too extreme; no, that would never do at all. *One must set a good example to these young people*, she thought. *Someone has to, for goodness' sake.*

'No doubt you'll be criticising *me* when Neil and the boys arrive, Rufus.' Lucie's eyes were sparking with anger as she leaned forwards towards her brother-in-law. Her outfit was more everyday high street than the boutique wear preferred by her sibling, Sister Veronica noticed, which probably reflected their incomes. 'As per usual. But I actually love my children and believe in hands-on parenting. So make all the jokes you want when they get here but I don't care, I'm going to carry on doing things my way. I don't believe in all this tough love shit and healthy neglect you lot like to bandy around.' Lucie's husband Neil and children Ryan and Nathan were due to arrive at any time, their tardiness – Florence had explained – due to a rugby match in Milton Keynes that both boys had played in. 'Anyway, you don't even have children, so what gives you the right to dictate how they should be brought up?'

'Oh God, Germaine Greer's arrived,' Rufus snorted. 'Didn't realise I was coming to a feminist rally.'

Araminta shrieked with laughter.

'She's always been like that, haven't you, Luce?' she said.

'Always taking life a bit too seriously. Like the short hair by the way, did you choose convenience over style with that one?'

'Well at least I don't look like a drunk pig who's been stuffed into a corset,' Lucie spat back. 'Alcohol does contain so many calories, don't you find, Araminta?'

'Girls, girls, settle down.' Giles' eyes were amused, as he leaned forward towards his nieces, his huge belly pushing against the table. 'I like watching a cat fight as much as the next man, but it's Christmastime, hey? I once held a party for my staff at the Cheval Blanc Villa, you know, the elite hotel owned by that Saudi businessman Ahmad? He's a good friend of mine actually. I could tell you some stories about the devilish things we've got up to together in the past but I won't as ladies are present.' His laugh was filled with undisguised smuttiness.

Sister Veronica shifted in her seat, purposefully not looking at him, correcting the positon of her knife and fork on her plate loudly.

'Two of the secretaries got into an actual fist fight on the dance floor,' Giles said. 'It was beyond hilarious. They were sloshed, of course. I'd been feeding them Dom Perignon all evening, had to get them all sozzled as that's part of the fun of the whole thing – seeing who will end up with who at the end of the night. Apparently, one had told a joke that the other had taken offence to. My goodness, you should have seen them go at it. Blood was drawn, it was fantastic – I can't tell you how us chaps enjoyed watching it unfold. I actually took bets on who would win. Ah, that really was a great night.' He broke off again to chuckle. 'But now it's nearly Christmas, so let's hold back on the fisticuffs until at least Boxing Day shall we, ladies?' He looked around at the assembled company, a wicked grin breaking out across his meaty face.

Maud giggled, while staring into the middle distance.

'You two always annoy each other,' she said. 'Don't you, girls?'

Great Saints, Sister Veronica thought, watching Maud. *What a pointless comment. Will no one tell these two grown women to shut up and act their age? They both must be in their forties. It's like a zoo here, everyone braying and snorting whenever they please. Give me the convent dinner table any day. Even putting up with Sister Irene's Bible quotations is better than listening to this spite and bile being thrown around by adults, who frankly, should know better.*

'I see you've had the place redecorated, Giles. Yet again.' Cecily cleared her throat and looked around her, pursing her lips. 'Not to my taste, if I'm honest.' Sister Veronica briefly raised her eyes to the ceiling. *Here we go again*, she thought.

'Well, business is doing brilliantly at the moment.' Giles smiled, enjoying his sister-in-law's disapproval. 'The profits of Beresford's Breaded Wonders just keep flying in. And Flo likes to keep the place looking bright, don't you, darling?'

'Sorry?' Florence took a moment to respond as she lifted her gaze from the table. 'What did you say, Giles?' *She didn't hear a word her husband had just said about his secretaries fighting*, Sister Veronica thought. *Probably used to listening to stories like that. I don't know how she puts up with him, arrogant fool.*

'I'm *so* glad the fish finger business is booming,' Cecily said, her mouth puckering. 'You must be proud, Giles, to have built up such a *worthy* empire over the years.'

'I am top of my game at the moment.' Giles licked his lips, ignoring Cecily's digs as much as he was ignoring his wife's sickly countenance. 'Never been better, in actual fact. No thanks to the idiot manager I fired last month, he was dragging his feet and I don't need any dead wood on the team. You should have seen the look on his face when I gave him his marching orders, thought the spineless wimp was actually going to blub.'

Maud smiled at Giles, focusing her gaze on him, apparently finding his egotistical self-image very acceptable.

'Oh, by the way,' Lucie said, turning towards her uncle. 'Neil and I are actually vegetarians. I have told you and Auntie Florence this several times, but no one ever seems to listen and bother to prepare suitable food. And the boys are pescatarians. Although I never buy them fish fingers, only fresh salmon and sea bass. Just thought it worth mentioning. Again. I obviously only ate the veg today. I've brought a frozen nut roast with me, and I'm going to ask Mrs Hardman to cook it for my family on Christmas Day.' Sister Veronica watched Araminta roll her eyes at this piece of news. Rita Hardman, Florence had explained to Sister Veronica, was a local woman from Little Ashby who'd been with the family for years. She was clearly going to have her work cut out feeding this mob on the twenty-fifth. *If nothing else*, Sister Veronica thought, *she was going to enjoy piling on a few more pounds during her stay.*

'You're such a fucking hippy, Luce,' Araminta slurred, draining her fourth glass. 'Maybe that's why you're so miserable, you need a nice fat juicy steak to cheer you up.'

'Rare,' Rufus snorted. 'Literally dripping in blood, to get her iron levels back to normal.'

'Or you could just donate some of your fat to me,' Lucie said, her voice a snarl. 'The pair of you have enough blubber to coat a school of whales.'

Sister Veronica stood up, smoothing down her habitually worn long-sleeved shirt and tweed skirt. Like all the nuns in her convent, she hadn't donned a habit for years.

'Thank you all for a lovely evening,' she said, placing her napkin in a neat heap to the left of her plate. 'The food really was excellent, I'll have to tell Mrs Hardman when I see her, and I hope you all enjoy the pudding. I'm afraid I've developed a headache, so if you'll excuse me I'm going to go and find a quiet corner to rest in.' *And I can't stand another minute of this obnoxious tittle-tattling*, she added to herself, taking care to keep her expression bland. She was, after all, a guest, and had been brought up with enough manners to know how to behave in company, unlike many of the heathens present. But in her mind she was there for Florence and no one else, and from now on intended to limit her exposure to the rabble's endless tiresome conflict as much as possible.

'I'll come with you.' Florence pushed back her chair and stood up, as various sentiments were called from around the table.

'It's like having Mother Teresa staying with us,' Sister Veronica heard Rufus whisper loudly as she exited the room. 'At least we can swear properly now.'

Maud's silly chuckle annoyed her more than Rufus' words.

She exhaled as she walked down the oak-panelled corridor, glancing over to her cousin, her skirt's waistband feeling significantly tighter than it had earlier.

'I'm so sorry, V,' Florence said, using her old pet name for her, looking back. 'That lot are a damned nightmare, I know they are. They're always the same when they get together, snapping, backbiting, trying to outdo each other. It's so embarrassing but none of them seem to care. I never know what to do about it, they don't listen to a word I say. If I try to intervene and introduce some good manners they just make fun of me. And God knows where we went wrong with Coco, I sometimes think she needs a good slap.'

'Sometimes a good hard shock works wonders,' Sister Veronica murmured. 'Although teenage girls seem rife with hormones these days, more so than when we were young. Don't fret too much, Flo, there's no reason why Coco won't grow into a fine young lady eventually. And it must be hard for her, her parents fighting so much. Perhaps it's having more of an effect on her than anyone realises.'

Florence shook her head. *She seems to be shrinking as she walks,* Sister Veronica thought, taking in her cousin's bowing shoulders, and stooped back. *She looks so much older than me now. What on earth is wrong? It can't just be the ghastly relatives.*

'Flo, listen,' she said, stopping in the big hall in front of the old oak front door. She looked around, checking they were alone. 'Why did you really invite me here? I can see something's bothering you, but I can't help you unless you tell me what it is.'

Florence also stopped, bringing her pale, puffy gaze to meet Sister Veronica's.

'Oh, V, there is something actually,' she said, her mouth trembling. 'I'm so sorry, I did really want to see you, catch up like old times and all that. But something terrible has been going on and I didn't know who to turn to. I racked my brain and tried to think of the most trustworthy person I know, and if I'm completely honest you were the only person who sprang to mind. You're the only person I know who has a thoroughly good heart. And I can't talk to any of these idiots.' She gestured back down the corridor towards the dining room. 'For obvious reasons. None of the selfish lot of them have ever been any good at giving advice, apart from Wilfred, and he's still a child. Maud's pretty harmless, and Lucie's not too bad when you get her away from Araminta. Those two always bring out the worst in each other. But I can't talk to her, not about this.'

Sister Veronica smiled. *Now we're getting somewhere,* she thought.

'Florence, I'm glad you think I might be able to help,' she said gently. 'Now why don't you tell me what's troubling you.'

'Right.' Florence breathed out, her eyes a shade brighter. 'Well, you see—'

DING, the doorbell rang.

Voices could be heard outside.

Sister Veronica smiled at her cousin's frustrated expression.

'Why don't you answer that, Florence? We have all evening to talk,' she said. 'I promise we'll make some time later, I'll make sure of it.'

'I'm so sorry, V, it must be Lucie's Neil and the boys.' Florence walked over to the door. 'There's always something going on in this house at the moment, I never get a moment's peace.' She arranged her face into a dutifully welcoming expression, undid the bolts, turned the key and opened the door.

The most stunning young lady Sister Veronica had ever seen stood quietly on the doorstep, dressed in an elegant Chanel suit. Behind her was a man who was wheeling two suitcases towards the door, and to the right of her, holding on very tightly to her hand, was a frightened-looking young boy.

'Ophelia,' Florence breathed, seeming momentarily thrown. 'How lovely to see you. I'm so sorry, my dear, I forgot you were arriving this evening. Do come in.'

'I phoned this morning and spoke to Giles. He said it would be fine for us to arrive a day earlier than we'd planned,' the young woman said in perfect tones. 'I just presumed he'd pass the news on to you?'

'He probably did, and it probably escaped my head for the merest second.' Florence smiled, ushering the party in towards the warm. 'You know what us old ladies are like, memories like sieves. Of course it's fine for you to arrive today, Ophelia. Please, come in and make yourself at home.'

Sister Veronica absentmindedly stepped to one side as the new guests made their way into the hall. For a moment, she became lost in thought as she gazed at the faint bluish-purple bruise around Ophelia's eye. The girl had tried to hide it with make-up, of course, but the mark covered a large area and its colours were too deep to be fully hidden for long. Florence, now busy bustling around and bending down to welcome the little boy, didn't seem to have noticed it, or wasn't showing any signs of doing so. With a rush of cold air, the man who'd arrived with Ophelia swished the cases inside and closed the door.

'Oh, Veronica, let me introduce you to Ophelia and Sam.' Florence smiled as she stood up, arms outstretched around the pair. 'Ophelia is our niece, my brother Tarquin's daughter, God rest his soul. And I'm very pleased to introduce you to my darling cousin, Sister Veronica,' she said to Ophelia. 'And this,' she said, nodding to the tall man now training his dark eyes onto Sister Veronica, 'is Digby.'

2

Sister Veronica met the hooded gaze of the man standing before her. His eyes really were the blackest she'd ever encountered, which was funny really because when you observed them properly they were actually a dark hazel colour. But on first sight, they appeared to resemble the hollow black holes of a skeleton. *Come now, Veronica*, she had a quick word with herself. *Just because you've spotted a bruise on Ophelia's face, doesn't mean you should immediately jump to any conclusions. There might be a perfectly good explanation for the injury, she may have hurt herself in an accident, walked into a door, or something else equally innocuous. Give poor Digby a chance before you start comparing him to a dead body. For goodness' sake, don't give in to this awful feeling of doom you've been having, just try and help the family have a nice Christmas together.*

'Good to meet you, Sister.' Digby gave her hand a shake. His hand was weak, limp and slightly sweaty. 'I'm from a Catholic family myself.'

'Ah wonderful,' Sister Veronica said more enthusiastically than she felt. The traumatic events of a year ago – when she'd become embroiled in the investigation of a horrific murder –

still affected her, and she would never forget the disillusionment she'd felt upon stumbling on the corrupt private lives of several well-respected priests. The vast gulf between the ideology presented by some, and the actuality of their personal choices had shaken her faith in her church, and she now practised a private faith based on reverence of the universe, or God, or love or whatever you wanted to call it, and took all the dogma with newly opened eyes.

Digby, she saw, was watching her as much as she was taking him in. *Well, this could be interesting*, she thought. *We are both observers. A potentially potent combination. But what are we thinking about each other? Well, I know what I'm thinking, or trying to think about him, but why is he so interested in me? I'm just a harmless little old nun, surely.* She took in the man's brown-and-grey hair, which was several inches long and brushed back into a wolfish point. His nose, a giant affair, sat in pride of place above his small mouth and gently receding chin. There was a sense of weakness about him which was in tension with an intense personal control, brought to Sister Veronica's attention as she watched his actions. He took off his coat in a robotic manner, before smoothing down all the sides, picking off any errant fluff and hairs that had become attached to it during his journey. Then he nodded at Ophelia and Sam to do the same. When they'd finished, a process done in silence, Digby laid the coat in Florence's outstretched arms with the care of someone passing a baby at a christening, never smiling once, then motioned to the other two to do the same.

'Would you like some dinner?' Florence said, shifting the coats in her arms so she could motion down the corridor to the dining room. Raucous laughs and loud reproaches could be heard from behind the closed door. 'There's more than enough left. Do come and sit down at the table, the others will have to shift up and make room for you.'

Ophelia and Sam both immediately looked at Digby. He gave a very small shake of his head, so slight it was barely perceptible.

'Would it be all right if we have something to eat in the kitchen tonight, Florence?' Ophelia said. 'We don't want to make any extra work for you, and I think Sam's a bit too tired to sit with everyone after the journey.'

'Absolutely, no problem at all.' Florence bustled off down a different corridor. 'Follow me, and I'll get you settled. I'll take your cases up to your room while you're eating. You can have the peach room.'

'Thank you.' Ophelia, looking relieved, stepped lightly after her aunt without glancing at her husband, Sam clinging tightly to her hand all the time. Digby lined up the two suitcases he'd brought in until they were standing exactly next to each other, before following his family, his strides deliberate, almost swaggering, in a way that was at odds with his weak handshake. *Gracious, what an intriguing match those two are*, Sister Veronica thought as she watched his back view disappear. *Ophelia's well-tailored and beautiful, the kind of woman who should have so many options open to her in life, yet she seems strangely held in Digby's thrall. He's awkward and very closed, and there's something odd about him. Well, if this house is good for nothing else, it's a prime spot for people-watching, and I've always loved doing that.*

Not wanting to bump in to any other members of the household for a while, and knowing that her cousin was now busy settling the new arrivals in, Sister Veronica hovered in the large, semicircular hall, wondering if it would be best if she went back to her room – the blue room – to rest. But remembering her promise to Florence to continue their conversation, she circumvented the magnificent Christmas tree, breathing in a delicious waft of pine needles, to stare at the portraits of Florence and Giles' ancestors that hung in heavy gilt frames on the wall. *A rum lot*, she thought. *Not a group of smilers, that was for sure. But very well dressed and imposing.*

The entrance hall, an arresting half-moon space, had several doors and corridors fanning off it that led to different parts of the big house, as well as a staircase that curled up and away to the first floor. Sister Veronica looked around at the space that could have been so welcoming and inviting, but instead, still held the austere coldness she remembered from her childhood. She'd always been too scared to go upstairs alone then, asking her mother to accompany her to her room, or waiting for one of the cousins to lead the way. The house had always seemed a place of ghostly memories not quite put to rest; the severe portraits, the dark walls, the dim corridor lights, the abandoned back living room – now unused and forgotten – that mad old Henrietta used to hold court in. But perhaps that was just her overactive imagination, she thought. Her mind went to the current family, all alive and well, most of them braying and shouting at each other. So many people were in the house she sometimes had to take stock of who belonged to who. There was Florence and Barnaby, of course, children of mad old Henrietta. Their younger brother Tarquin had lost his life to cancer several years ago, bless his soul, his wife Marina following him to the next life soon after. Magnus, Florence and Giles' only son, had two children, Coco and Wilfred. Barnaby and Cecily had two children, Araminta and Lucie, and Lucie and Neil had the boys, Ryan and Nathan. And then beautiful Ophelia, Tarquin and his wife's adopted daughter, who'd lost both her parents young, and her little boy, Sam. And then old Maud, Giles' cousin, who didn't have a partner or children. So including Digby, Rufus and herself there would be eighteen of them at the house for Christmas. Gracious, quite the gathering. The constant company would take some getting used to. She turned her attention to the decorations on the tree, finding a warmth and comfort in their familiar festive designs, wondering what the dear sisters were doing in their Soho convent back in London.

Then a door opened somewhere, and she heard two low muttered voices. Immediately curious, but not wanting to be seen, she stayed very still, hardly daring to breathe.

'Don't start all that again.' It was Giles, his low voice sounding a lot less jovial than at dinner. 'I've had enough of it. And at the dinner table too. Anyone could have heard. Terribly bad form.'

'Well *stop it* then,' Rufus' voice said, his tone frustrated. 'I know what you're up to, Giles, and I've already told you to stop but you didn't listen. You need to make it right. Things are going to get bad for you if you ignore me again.' He was talking louder than Giles, probably due to the wine, Sister Veronica thought.

'Godammit, keep your voice down, man,' Giles hissed. 'I've told you before, you've got it all wrong. And how dare you come into my house and threaten me. Who do you think you are? I'll tell you, you're a rogue, and I've a good mind to throw you out right now.'

'Then you'd have to explain why you did that to everyone else, wouldn't you?' Rufus' voice was angry now. 'But honesty has never been your best attribute has it, Giles? That's been proven extensively. By all means, throw me out. And I'll take great pleasure in telling everyone what you've been up to.'

Giles growled, saying nothing.

'I'll give you until tomorrow evening,' Rufus said. 'And no longer. You need to make this right, Giles, and if you don't then–'

Another door opened and faster footsteps came down a corridor.

'Giles?' Florence's tired voice called. 'Darling, is that you? Do come to the kitchen and say hello to Ophelia, Digby and Sam, they've just arrived. I can't remember you saying that they were coming today, but maybe you did. My head's so foggy at the moment.'

'I'll be there in a moment, dear,' Giles called, his voice lighter. He said something low to Rufus that Sister Veronica didn't catch, then his footsteps could be heard getting closer as he approached the hall. The corridor leading to the kitchen also led off the main entrance hall and Sister Veronica started up the staircase at once, not wanting Giles to know she'd overheard anything. Reaching the top step, she padded along the soft carpet to her bedroom, thinking hard. So a family secret was revealing itself already. Dash it all, she'd been hoping the sixth sense feeling she'd been suffering wouldn't come to anything, but now it pulsated with strength throughout her body and mind. Rufus had been accusing Giles of some sort of wrongdoing. Was whatever they'd been referring to the matter upsetting Florence so much? Aware of her promise to her cousin that they would find a time to chat later that evening, Sister Veronica opened her bedroom door, wondering if she would ever be able to talk to Florence privately with so many relatives swarming around. She'd have to find a way, she decided. Florence had been so close to disclosing whatever it was, they'd just need a few more minutes alone together, and she'd make that happen one way or another.

3

Ophelia closed her eyes. She was listening to Digby reprimand Sam for his lack of table manners. The poor boy was only four for Christ's sake, he was doing his best. But there was no point in her intervening at this stage, she had learnt from bitter experience only to fight the bigger battles, the ones that compromised her and Sam's safety in some way.

She thought back to when she'd first had a conversation with Digby, at a work Christmas do at a Covent Garden pub in London. They'd both been working at McBain's Publishers then, she was still getting over her recent split with Danny the wannabe musician, and had made a vow to herself that her next boyfriend would not be another charming sex-pot with an alcohol problem who was always a little bit more interested in becoming famous and getting another drink than he was in her. She'd just turned thirty and had a deep yearning to settle down with a steady partner and start a family. This desire had turned into a bit of an obsession, and her longing for a child had become overwhelming. She suspected that the fact she was adopted and had always felt like she never really properly belonged to her family may have something to do with wanting a family of her very own so badly; a unit to belong to that wanted her as much as she wanted them. But most of the men she knew were still happy playing the field, very vocal about how they were no way ready for children, and her last two boyfriends had been a lot of fun, when they were sober, but not marriage material.

Then she met Digby. He worked on a different floor in McBains, a tall Victorian building in Pimlico. She'd passed him a few times in the corridor, and he'd always looked serious, never smiling at her, and they'd never actually been introduced or had any reason to speak. The Christmas party night was different. Digby, on his second glass of red wine, seemed like a different person to the solemn man she'd seen before. He was smiling at a silly story someone was telling, still quiet, but obviously enjoying himself. She caught him staring in her direction a few times. Usually if a man did this – in her experience – their next move would be to come over and talk to her, try to charm her with their drunken ramblings. But Digby didn't, just stayed where he was, shooting her the occasional glance. Once he smiled at her and gave a little wave. Ophelia had found his reticence strangely attractive, attributing it to a deeper sense of chivalry and shyness in him.

An hour later, emboldened by the two vodka and lemonades she'd drunk, she'd worked her way across through her drunken colleagues to where Digby was standing. It was out of character for her to be so forward, but something in his reticence made her bold.

'So, I hear your name is Digby?' she'd said with her best ravishing smile. Their conversation had lasted for the rest of the night, and she'd been struck by his knowledge of the world and interest in literature. Danny had hated reading, always lying on top of her book if she'd tried to read a chapter or two in bed, pulling silly faces at her until with a sigh she'd closed the book and given her full attention to him. But Digby was different, she'd never met anyone like him before and she'd been entranced. Especially when he'd said he wasn't interested in short relationships, and that he was looking for a long-term, permanent partner. She could tell he was interested by the way his eyes didn't leave her from the moment she'd struck up conversation. *Could this be it?* she'd thought to herself. *Could Digby and I be soulmates?* Now, six years later, she knew that the answer to that question was no. But Digby now had a hold over her that no one else knew about. She was trapped in his clutches and there was nothing she or anyone else could do about it. She just had to keep playing his game, and try not to go completely mad.

She opened her eyes. Sam's face was white, anxious, staring at her, imploring her to say something. Digby was saying that he was going to sit there and eat the last quarter of the sandwich on his plate, even if it took hours.

'Well, I don't think we have to stuff Sam so full of food that he throws up like last time,' Ophelia said lightly, standing up. 'He has such a slight build, his stomach's probably not that big. Come on, Sam, let's go and get you settled for the night.'

Digby narrowed his eyes but said nothing, remembering what had happened three nights before, when he'd made him sit and eat every single vegetable and potato left on his plate. It had taken two and a half hours until he'd stuffed the last piece of broccoli in, and then the little boy had stood up and immediately vomited his meal on to the floor, before bursting into hysterical tears as he thought his daddy would tell him off. Ophelia had been the one who'd cleared the mess up, put Sam to bed, sneaked him up half a sandwich so he didn't go to sleep hungry while Digby was roaring about how the boy had misbehaved and should go to bed on an empty stomach. She always tried to give Sam small meals, giving him secret snacks in between. But Digby liked to give him a full plate, then taunt him with tales of how when he was a boy, he wasn't allowed to leave the table without eating every single thing, and received a rap on the knuckles if he ate too slowly. Florence had made Sam a very generous cheese sandwich with thick slices from a farmhouse loaf, obviously trying to be kind and feed the boy well. But Ophelia's stomach had sunk at the sight of it, knowing what was going to happen. No matter, her and Sam were up and away from the table now. She hoped Digby would stay downstairs while she put their lovely boy to bed, giving her and Sam a chance to spend much appreciated time alone together. She took her son's hand and led him towards the door.

'Don't undermine me in front of the child,' Digby hissed in her ear, making her jump. 'You always do that. The problem with you is that you have no logic, no reasoning. Sam needs to toughen up and you keep getting in the way of it, like always. Your parenting is awful, the boy has no hope. But then we know how useless you are, don't we, Ophelia?'

Ophelia marched straight on, pulling Sam behind her. She'd heard it all before many times, and Digby's words no longer made her obviously upset. They just added to the intense feelings of dread and fear that had paralysed her insides for the last four years, that had been there so long she'd got used to them. It had been hard enough to get him to come to Chalfield Hall, he always said he hated her family, that they were all lunatics with no common sense. She'd expected him to treat her badly as a punishment, because that's how he operated. It seemed her fears would be realised. The only way she'd got him to agree to the visit was by reminding him how much they could inherit one day, if they kept in Florence and Giles' good books. Money was like a carrot on a stick to Digby, he always wanted more of it but never seemed to be able to earn the amount he desired from his own work.

'There we go,' she said soothingly to Sam, as they walked up the corridor. 'Let's go and find the bedroom Florence has given to us. Doesn't the peach room sound lovely?' She often hoped her feeling of dread wasn't in some way transferred to her son, that she was protecting him from what was going on between her and Digby as much as possible. She knew he lacked confidence and was scared of his father, but every day she tried to fill him with as much joy and love as she could. She hoped this would be enough for Sam to grow up happy.

Digby stood watching his wife and boy leave, his hands in his pockets. It was only right that he punished Ophelia, he knew, because of what she'd done four years before. He would never forgive her for that. And far from receding, his feelings of resentment and detestation towards her were getting stronger as the days passed. He knew what he was going to do next.

4

Sister Veronica smiled. Wilfred had been telling her about different types of dinosaurs for the last half an hour and her head was reeling with all the intricate facts he'd imparted. She felt quite dizzy with her new knowledge about the size of the Apatosaurus, the feeding habits of Velociraptors, the German name for the Archaeopteryx, and the carnivorous tendencies of the Megalosaurus. She was hoping that he would stop talking so intently at her soon, the boy had hardly taken a breath and left no room for her to contribute to the conversation, but there was something rather appealing about his innocence – much younger than his fifteen years – and enthusiasm so she did her best to keep nodding with interest at his endless Cretaceous and Jurassic details while her eyes scanned the room.

She and Wilfred were sitting on the chaise longue in the corner of the large front living room. She'd dared to brave the throng again after hearing voices collect downstairs. The brief rest on her bed had done her the world of good, and she was now ready for another instalment of family life. She could always sneak away for more respite later if needs be.

Various points of soft lighting made this room much cosier than the rest of the house, she thought, where dark oak panels, small windows and narrow passageways abounded. Lucie's husband Neil had arrived with their two boys Ryan and Nathan a little while ago. The two tall lads, still clad in their muddy rugby clothes, had grunted greetings at the assembled throng before sinking into a sofa. Lucie had fussed around them initially, getting them snacks and drinks – apparently they'd had a McDonald's dinner en route, Filet-O-Fish burgers, of course, and a spicy bean wrap for Neil – ignoring Rufus' jibes that she was a helicopter parent. The two boys hadn't looked up from their phones since.

Neil wore the same expression of resigned defeat Sister Veronica feared had been on her own face during dinner, as he chatted to his wife by the grand piano. It was a look that said, 'I'm here and I'm going to put up with your insane relatives for as long as I can, Lucie, because I love you, but I'd rather be at work, or watching paint dry, or on the moon, or literally anywhere else away from your family.' Every now and again his eyes flicked over to the loudly braying Araminta who was sitting on a pouf by her husband, at which point he ran a hand through his short black hair, a gesture of frustration, if Sister Veronica was correct.

Rufus was now the picture of drunken bonhomie, the top buttons of his expensive paisley shirt now undone. He was in the middle of telling a story about a friend of his who'd gone clubbing with his son and had got so drunk he'd ended up dancing on a podium in a nightclub, and Sister Veronica reflected that no one on earth would guess that he'd had such serious angry words with Giles just an hour before. Maud and Digby, sitting on a sofa nearby, were smiling politely at Rufus' monologue. Maud had her usual knitting in her hands, she'd already explained to Sister Veronica that she liked to knit babies' booties and jackets and donate them to her local charity shop. A worthy cause. Hopefully all the babies in need of footwear were female as blue wool didn't appear to be part of Maud's repertoire, Sister Veronica mused. Cecily, near to them, was looking less amused at Rufus' tale and Barnaby had nodded off in an armchair, his mouth now sagging open.

Another large Christmas tree stood by the window, its golden lights sparkling across the tastefully arranged decorations. For a moment, Sister Veronica felt a surge of contentment. Perhaps the festive season would be enjoyable after all, she thought. Seeing her family together like this near the tree, laughing and sipping drinks, had sparked a little warm feeling in her insides. Yes, they all had their peculiarities, but didn't everyone, when it came down to it? Perhaps they'd got all their arguing out of the way over dinner, and were now settling down to some quality family time. Maybe she'd judged many of them too harshly. After all, everyone had light and dark in them and now she was seeing more of the light and love coming out. Big personalities? Certainly. But people with good in them too. She couldn't hear what Coco was saying to Magnus on the opposite side of the room, which was a blessing, as the girl's voice was so gratingly relentless. Perhaps she'd calmed down now and wasn't demanding something for once. For the first time in days, the feeling of impending doom inside of her ebbed slightly.

Florence came bustling into the room holding a tray of glasses containing a pale-yellow liquid. She looked a bit brighter than at dinner, Sister Veronica thought. Perhaps the very fact she'd begun to share her troubles had lifted a small weight from her mind.

'Who's for vermouth?' Florence said as she proffered the drinks forward. Several glasses immediately found themselves in the hands of assorted guests. Even Wilfred took one, to no objection from his father. 'Has anyone seen Giles?' Florence continued, looking around. 'I need him to help me fix the lock on the back door. It keeps sticking and he's usually the only one who can get the key to turn.'

Met with no new information on her husband's whereabouts, Florence turned and left the room, the now empty tray tucked under her arm. Sister Veronica hugged her apple juice to her chest, having been the only person not to have taken a glass. Memories of her time in Somerset – when the baby in her charge had been abducted as she sipped elderflower champagne – still kept her awake some nights, and she'd vowed not to touch a drop of alcohol since. With Wilfred now concentrating on his beverage, the dinosaur tutorial apparently over, she took the opportunity of heaving herself up and padding out of the room after her cousin.

'Flo,' she called down the corridor to the kitchen. 'Do you have a minute? Perhaps we could have that chat now?'

Florence's scream, she later reflected, was a sound she'd never be able to erase from her memory. It was high-pitched and animalistic, a noise filled with terror and pain. Bombing into the kitchen as fast as she could, she took in the scene within seconds.

Giles, his eyes rolling back in his head, was staggering around the room, his movements jerky and uncontrolled. Suddenly, a huge stream of vomit exited his mouth and he spun round on a downwards vortex, crashing heavily on to the floor. By the time she'd reached him he was prostrate on the kitchen tiles, his face turned to the side. His mouth was open and only the whites of his eyes were showing. The twitching died away and in seconds he was lying very still. Florence, her hands to her mouth, was completely frozen a few feet away from him. Sister Veronica bent down, grabbing Giles' wrist.

'I can't feel a pulse, Flo,' she muttered, pressing hard between the bone and the tendon. Multiple footsteps came pounding along the corridor and soon Lucie and Neil's shocked faces were at the door, with Cecily's soon joining them.

'I'll call an ambulance,' Lucie said quickly, reaching for her phone, retrieving it with dexterity from her pocket and punching in the nines.

Ten minutes later Giles and Florence had been whisked away by paramedics to Northampton Hospital. The remaining party sat silently in the living room, or stood quietly in the kitchen, waiting for news.

'Could be a heart attack,' Rufus said gruffly as he leaned over to switch the kettle on. Sister Veronica eyed him, saying nothing. 'Old boy eats far too much fatty food, always has done. Aunt Florrie said his blood pressure went through the roof last year.'

Yes, but you would say that wouldn't you, she thought, watching his face. *When only a little while ago I heard you threatening the man. But you were in the living room when Giles was found in the kitchen. And so were Cecily and Barnaby, who very much want Giles out of here. I felt in my old bones that something was very wrong in this house the moment I arrived, and now this has happened. Dash, why did that feeling have to be right? And why has it not gone now, in fact, it seems to have become stronger? I'll be keeping an eye on all of you from now on. Surely nothing else can happen. Poor Florence, this is quite enough awfulness for one Christmas.*

She turned away from him, busying herself by collecting mugs together, hoping she was wrong to have suspicions about the family members and that Florence would call soon with good news.

5

'I'm bored,' Coco said, her voice gratingly whiny. She kicked the leg of the piano stool underneath her, then carelessly bashed out a few notes. Sister Veronica winced. 'Daddy, listen to me. I'm *really* bored. Can you give me your credit card so I can do some online shopping? Daddy! Can you even hear what I'm saying?' Her hair, drawn up today in an elaborate design on top of her head, fell down in ringlets around her kohl-blackened eyes.

Sister Veronica stared at the girl, wondering if she would successfully keep her disbelief from showing. It was the day after Giles' collapse, and a group of them sat in the living room, trying to absorb the terrible news that despite the paramedics' and doctors' best efforts, Giles had been pronounced dead shortly after his arrival at hospital. Coco had showed no signs of sadness at the departure of her grandfather other than a shrug and a comment about what a pity it was, and was managing to still be entirely self-absorbed. It was almost fascinating, the fact that she tried to make every situation about herself and seemingly had no care for anyone else. Sister Veronica thought it might be best if she sat on her hands in case she tried to strangle the girl.

Florence had rung the house to impart the news of her husband's death the previous evening, hardly able to speak, her words constricted as though it hurt to utter them. Neil had gone straight to the hospital to collect her, being the only person with a car who was not immensely drunk, and Sister Veronica had gone, too, desperately wanting to comfort her cousin. Florence had stared into space during the journey back to Chalfield Hall, and the tears had come the minute the front door was closed behind her. Sister Veronica had stayed up until the early hours of the morning, her arms round her cousin, saying anything she could think of that might soothe the shock and pain. At some point they'd both fallen asleep on the sofa, and when she'd opened her eyes shortly after half past seven, Florence was no longer there.

Now, Sister Veronica blinked, her eyes stinging with tiredness. Through the window she could see Neil and his boys practising rugby throws on the front lawn, yelling to each other and laughing when one dropped the ball, never seeming to run out of energy, apparently unable to feel the freezing air. Ryan and Nathan were nice boys, shy in front of adults, but with good hearts and very healthy, she thought, what with their near continuous exercise. Even if they were a bit mollycoddled by their parents, who were always running around making sure they had enough to eat and drink. *So normal life carries on amidst a crisis, yet again. And a good thing too. It's the day before Christmas Eve today. The children should all be excited, not that there's much chance of that with this motley crew. I wonder if any of us have enough energy to give them some sort of Christmas now? We'll have to, I suppose, one way or another.*

Watching the boys' activity made her think of the still-sleeping Maud. When on earth is that woman going to get up?

she wondered. Lucie had told her that Maud loved lie-ins and rarely rose before midday. Mrs Hardman was due to arrive any minute to start the lunch, and she would want to know how many she was cooking for. Giles' cousin's slovenly habit irritated her; goodness gracious, at the convent one only stayed in bed all day if one was suffering from the direst of illnesses. Failing one of them you went to morning chapel every day or faced Mother Superior's wrath.

Turning back to the room, she watched as Coco, having received no response from her father – who was in an inert heap on the sofa, his glazed eyes staring into the middle distance – stood up from her perch on the piano stool and walked towards him, her eyebrows raised and her eyes bulging.

'Hello?' she said, her voice getting louder. 'Is anyone at home? Earth to Daddy?' In one swift movement she hit his head with the palm of her hand, the force being sufficient enough to push his head right back against his neck.

'What?' Magnus murmured, looking up at her, his hand immediately going to his throat.

'I said, give me your credit card,' Coco's words were loud, harsh.

'You silly little spoilt brat.' Lucie leaned forwards from her place on the sofa, a tray of steaming mugs on the coffee table in front of her. 'Is it possible for you to think about anyone else other than yourself for just one minute? Do you have any idea that your father's dad has just died? Imagine how he must be feeling. And we have no idea what caused it yet, one minute Giles was fine and the next he was lying on the kitchen floor. Do you think that perhaps, just for one day, you could leave your father alone and go and do something by yourself instead?' Lucie's eyes were gleaming as she leaned back. 'And I never want to see you hit anyone like that again.'

'But he's ignoring me.' Coco's voice became a shrill wail. 'I was just trying to get his attention. No one ever listens to me in this house. I hate you all, I wish I lived somewhere else.' With that, she turned and left the room, the habitual slam of the door marking her exit.

'The feeling's mutual,' Cecily muttered. She and Barnaby were sitting on another sofa, willingly drinking all the tea and coffee Sister Veronica and Lucie were making in tag-team style, without offering to make a round themselves. Sister Veronica glanced at her. *The terrible thing*, she thought as she heaved herself up, *is that if we hear news that Giles' death was not due to natural causes or accidental, then we all have to face the fact that one person among us is a murderer. And that is not a thought I relish at all. But let's cross that bridge if we come to it. As Rufus said, Giles did not lead the healthiest of lifestyles, and a heart attack may well have got him last night. I'm sure we'll find out soon.*

Making her way to the kitchen in the hope of finding Florence, she passed Rufus and Araminta in the hallway. They were standing very close together, talking quietly. Araminta was wearing sunglasses, despite the dull December day. Probably hungover, Sister Veronica concluded. Rufus took his wife's hand and led her up the spiral staircase. *Perhaps they're going to sleep off the after-effects*, she thought. *I'd be in a hospital bed if I ever drunk as much as they did last night. They must have built up a high tolerance to it.*

The only person in the kitchen turned out to be Wilfred. She glanced at the clock; it was nearly midday.

'Are you making something?' Sister Veronica approached the counter, now strewn with piles of paper, cardboard, glue, paint and an overflowing box of material scraps.

'Yes, I'm making dinosaur Christmas tree decorations.' Wilfred turned, pushing his glasses further up his nose. 'Everyone's so depressed today, I thought it might cheer them up.'

'What a lovely idea.' Sister Veronica eyed the very detailed and savage-looking Tyrannosaurus Rex depiction that Wilfred was gluing to red cardboard. 'You've certainly done the teeth well. Did they really have so much slobber coming out of their mouths?'

'It's quite possible,' Wilfred said. 'T-rexes were carnivores, and I'm a realist. I want to show them looking as natural as possible.'

'Well, I can see you're very busy, I'll let you get on.' Sister Veronica turned towards the door. 'Actually, I'm looking for your granny, have you seen her anywhere?'

'She's in the garden, crying.' Wilfred picked up a piece of tinsel. 'The phone rang and she answered it, and whatever the person said made Granny start doing loud snotty sobs.'

'Right.' Sister Veronica changed course and headed for the back door, marvelling at the boy's apparent dissociation from the current crisis and his grandmother's feelings. *Oh well, at least he was trying to make people happy with his ferocious drawings.*

She found Florence in the herb garden, surrounded by pots of sweet-smelling rosemary. She looked up as Sister Veronica approached, her face tear-stained and blotchy.

'There you are.' Sister Veronica sat down beside her on the small stone bench. 'You poor thing, Flo, it's all so much to take in. What a shock.'

'But that's not the worst of it.' Fresh tears sprang to Florence's eyes and her face crumpled. 'The coroner just phoned, V. Oh, this is so awful, I can hardly believe I'm going to say it. The autopsy was done early this morning and they found that the manner of death was poisoning. High levels of abrin were found in Giles. I'm not sure what that is but apparently it's deadly, very toxic. It seems that my husband was murdered, V. And it must have been by someone in the family, as we were the only ones here last night. The police will be arriving soon to investigate.'

Sister Veronica stared at her cousin, her mouth open, her

worst fears confirmed. Skin-crawling chills crept along the inside of her brain and she felt her heart begin to pound. So there *was* evil in the house. She'd suspected as much, felt some strange and worrying tensions as soon as she'd arrived, but had been hoping for the best, wanting her instincts to be wrong. She'd tried to ignore the awful feeling of impending badness, but now that this had happened she felt shaken to the core. Giles had been murdered and it justified her instincts. No, she did not like this one little bit, and the enormity of the danger they were all in with a killer in their midst hit her. She shook her head and reached out to hold her cousin's hand. She mustn't let on to Flo how terrified she felt, her cousin was already dealing with enough. The grief about her husband's demise seemed to have cushioned Florence's perception of the fact that one of the family was most likely a murderer. But why? Why would anyone go to such extreme lengths? It was important that she – Sister Veronica – outwardly displayed a sense of calm and clear-headedness, while inside she worked out the best way forward.

A rustle in some bushes near the house caught her attention. Footsteps ran up the path and the back door slammed. Sister Veronica's heart leapt so hard it hurt.

'Flo,' she said. 'I think someone was just listening to us. Now, if they heard what you just said this could be very serious. We may be in danger. You need to tell me everything you know about *anyone* who had a reason to harm Giles immediately. Don't leave anything out.'

6

Ophelia took the cup of tea Lucie was offering her and sat down. It was strange, she thought, settling back into the armchair and staring out of the window at the long drive, that Digby was spending so much more time with Sam nowadays. The two of them had left the house an hour earlier, with Digby saying the boy needed more fresh air and that Ophelia was stifling him with her overprotective motherly ways, not allowing him to romp about in the mud enough. Ophelia had thought it an unfair comment, particularly as she and Sam went for daily walks when Digby was at work, and spent a lot of time playing in the garden. She took the little boy to the Mini Shooter football club on Saturday mornings in term time, and in January he was due to start at a forest school where the children were encouraged to be outside as much as possible. But, as with most of Digby's taunts, she realised that replying and defending herself was futile. Because he wasn't interested in fact, he probably didn't actually care how much fresh air Sam got. His main aim was to belittle her in every way possible. And because of the bind Digby had her in, she had to find ways to bear this as well as she could.

'Isn't this all awful?' Lucie said, leaning forward. 'Giles could be a brute sometimes, but no one deserves to die just before Christmas. It's just too sad.'

'I know, I couldn't believe it when I woke up and Digby told me.' Ophelia was glad of the distraction. Too much of her time was spent trying to work out how to keep things calm for Sam and she often suffered from stress headaches. She turned and placed her cup down on the side table. It was nice being with other people for a change, even if it was under these awful circumstances. She felt safer, as though her relatives' presence diluted the atmosphere between Digby and her. It was why she'd wanted to come to Chalfield Hall so badly, just to be in a different place, with other people who wouldn't treat her the way her husband did. 'I must have fallen asleep with Sam, I'm always doing that. I missed everything that went on last night. Poor Giles.'

'And Florence is so heartbroken.' Lucie picked up a biscuit. She couldn't take her eyes from Ophelia's face; her bone structure was so perfect, her eyes so big, the lashes thick and long. She wondered why her cousin wore so much make-up, her foundation was literally plastered on today, she could see little clumps of it around her eyes. If she had Ophelia's face, Lucie decided, she wouldn't wear make-up at all. Not that she could be bothered with much at the best of times, just a bit of powder and mascara most days and lipstick if she was going out. Maybe Ophelia had low self-esteem or something, although God knows why. 'She was absolutely distraught at breakfast. I love your suit by the way. Is it Chanel?'

'Yes.' Ophelia nodded. 'Digby gave it to me. He chooses all my clothes.'

'Oh?' Lucie looked taken aback. She paused. 'Don't you buy any of your own things?'

'Not anymore.' Ophelia sighed. Lucie frowned.

The front door opened and a swirl of cold air filled the room. Footsteps could be heard in the hall.

'Mummy.' Sam rushed in and put his head on Ophelia's knee.

'Hello, darling,' Ophelia said, stroking his hair. 'Did you have a nice time with Daddy? You must have had a good walk, you were gone for a while.'

'Mummy.' Sam craned his head back and looked at her. 'Why do you always do everything wrong?'

'What?' A sick feeling entered Ophelia's chest. This sort of thing was happening more and more. 'Why did you say that, Sam?'

'Daddy says you do everything wrong,' Sam said. 'Why do you do that, Mummy?'

'I don't do everything wrong, Sam.' Ophelia lowered her gaze. It was awkward that Lucie was listening to this. She liked to keep her family problems away from everyone else in case they started asking questions. Digby didn't like people interfering. 'You don't have to believe Daddy when he says things like that.'

Lucie's eyes narrowed as she watched this exchange.

'Daddy says you are bad at driving.' Sam smiled, unaware of the impact his words were having on his mother and Lucie. 'And bad at spending money, bad at being my mummy, and a bad wife.'

'That's awful.' Lucie's voice was sharp. 'Your daddy shouldn't be saying things like that to you, Sam. You have a wonderful mummy, who loves you very much.'

Sam reached for a biscuit and turned away, apparently no longer in the mood for talking.

'It's fine, honestly,' Ophelia said in a low voice over his head. 'Digby's feeling a bit stressed with work at the moment, and he can say things he doesn't mean.'

'If Neil ever spoke to the kids about me like that I'd bag up his belongings, throw them on to the street and have the locks changed.' Lucie shifted position. 'It's just wrong, Ophelia, to make a child think badly of one of their parents. Unless that person is a terrible person, which you're not.'

'I know it sounds a bit strange but it's fine, really.' Ophelia glanced towards the door, nervousness in her eyes. She was wondering when Digby was going to come in, or whether he was outside listening to their conversation right now. 'Ah look, you still have your wellies on, Sam. Let's go into the hall and take them off. We don't want to get any mud on the carpet, do we?'

She stood up and led the little boy out of the room.

Lucie stared after her. What on earth had all that been about?

7

'Letters?' Sister Veronica repeated, the full focus of her stare on her cousin. 'What letters?' She was feeling a bit calmer now, the wave of terror having settled back down into muted fear. It was *so* important that she tried to think clearly. She made a huge effort to pull herself into some semblance of normality and to listen properly to what Flo had to tell her.

'Awful ones, V.' Florence's eyes filled up again. 'Really terrible. They've been arriving for over a year now, always hand delivered, no stamp on them, just waiting for me on the doormat when I come back from the village.'

They were sitting in the summer house at the end of the lawn, after deeming the herb garden too close to Chalfield Hall for comfort. From where they sat, Sister Veronica reckoned, they would have a good view of anyone wanting to overhear their words. She'd already made a comprehensive search round the sides and back of the summer house and was satisfied that they would hear the rustling if anyone tried to creep behind it, there were so many old leaves and rusty gardening equipment stashed there.

'And what on earth's in those letters?' Sister Veronica said.

'Well.' Florence wiped her eyes. 'The first one said, "THE LONGER YOU LEAVE IT, THE BIGGER THE PUNISHMENT". All written in capitals, so I didn't recognise the handwriting. I just thought it was a horrid joke when I first saw it, maybe one of the village teenagers playing a prank. I didn't take it seriously, and besides, I had no idea what the person was referring to. I still don't.'

'But then there were more letters?' Sister Veronica said.

'Yes, a lot more.' Florence shook her head. 'The second said something like, "YOU ARE IGNORING ME, NOTHING HAS CHANGED. STOP IT NOW, OR BAD THINGS WILL HAPPEN. YOU HAVE BEEN WARNED". Then after that, the letters became more frequent, two or three a week. They all contain threats, all telling us to stop doing something or terrible things will happen. Some are just insulting, calling us names, or saying we are incompetent liars, or things of that nature.'

'Oh, Flo,' Sister Veronica said. 'I'm so sorry, that sounds very stressful. What a bullying thing for someone to do. I hope you took the letters straight to the police?'

'I did at first.' Florence looked at her. 'A few weeks after they started arriving, I took them all to the police station in Northampton. They looked at them, and made a note of it, but they didn't take it that seriously. They said the majority of poison pen letters are purely malicious, with no proper criminal intent behind them, so they told us to ignore them and just carry on with our lives. The police kept the letters I'd brought and said to hand any more to them in case the sender became sloppy and accidentally identified themselves, which I did for a few months, but nothing came of it so in the end I started keeping them in a locked box in my room.'

'Not very helpful.' Sister Veronica grimaced. 'I'd like to take a look at the ones you have, if you don't mind?' *The sender must have unwittingly left a clue in them*, she thought. *People who think they're that clever often slip up, in one way or another.*

Florence nodded.

'Of course,' she said. 'I'd be so grateful for any help you can give, V. I've read them and reread them so many times, I can barely bring myself to look at the horrible things now.'

'Did you get any sense from them about who might be behind the letters?' Sister Veronica said. 'Any hints from what was written?'

'Well, strangely, the letters also included details about us that no one else should know,' Florence said. 'Private things, silly little facts that I didn't think anyone except Giles and I knew. Like when his blood pressure pills changed, and when I tripped over next door's cat and hurt my wrist. It must be someone who is very close to us, to know that kind of thing. And that's very upsetting. Oh, V, I know the family is generally a bunch of egomaniacs who don't have a social grace between them, but I never thought any of them would stoop to this, you know?'

Sister Veronica nodded. She felt the same. The notion that a member of one's own family was prepared to kill was stomach-churning, almost too disturbing to bear.

'And now you're worried that Giles' death has something to do with the person who wrote the letters?' she said.

'Yes.' Florence sniffed. 'Well, it makes sense, doesn't it? We get all these threats telling us to stop doing something or else, then suddenly my husband drops dead from abrin poisoning, whatever that is. That's why I invited everyone here for Christ-mas, V. I wanted everyone around me so I could feel safe. Protected. I just wanted to relax for once. And that's why I invited you; I thought if anyone could help me, it would be you. You've always been so sensible and clear-headed, even when we were children. I'm so sorry, I never thought anything like this would happen. It's all my fault Giles is dead, if I hadn't brought everyone together like this, he would probably still be alive.' Huge sobs overtook her, and for a few minutes, Sister Veronica held her cousin in her arms, letting the grief wash through her.

'Now listen to me, Flo,' she said, when Florence's breathing was slowing down again. 'It's not your fault at all, the only person responsible for Giles' death is whoever gave him abrin. I know this will be hard, but for now we are going to carry on as normal in front of the family, grieving, obviously, but normal other than that. We can't let people know we are suspicious, it might cause them to do something drastic. That includes Mrs Hardman, as she is also in and out of the house.'

'Oh, it wouldn't be her.' Florence managed a watery smile. 'Mrs Hardman has been with us for years. She's so reliable, so down to earth, if she wanted to do anything to the family she's had ample enough opportunity before. I trust her more than the rest of them put together, V.'

'No.' Sister Veronica shook her head. 'Unfortunately it could be any of them, Flo. Please believe me, it's really important that we don't talk about any of this to another soul. We don't know what else this person is planning to do, and any sign from us that we are looking for them could startle them into a reckless course of action.'

'All right.' Florence nodded, her smile replaced by anxiety. 'You're right, V. Gosh, this is going to be difficult.'

Sister Veronica gave her cousin a tight smile, wondering whether or not to share the awful feeling she'd had as soon as she'd arrived at Chalfield Hall. Rather than going away after Giles' demise, it had become stronger, more potent, as though the universe was trying to warn her about something else, a further catastrophe, encouraging her to be on high alert at all times. It was hard to describe the whole body–mind feeling, but it was one that made the hairs stand up on her arms, and an icy chill flood her brain. Sometimes it was weaker, sometimes stronger, but it was always there.

Just as she opened her mouth to say something, the sound of screeching tyres on the gravel to the front of the house made them both look around. A car door slammed.

'Oh no, that's all we need.' Florence sighed. 'Romilly's here. Magnus' ex-wife. She drives like a rally racer. Goes through several new tyres a year.'

Sister Veronica sat up. *Now this could be interesting*, she thought. *A new ingredient thrown into the already turbulent mix. Of course, Romilly is under suspicion as much as everyone else, it sounds like she's here enough. But the question is, will anyone slip up and provide us with a clue as to what in Great Saints is actually going on in this house?* She'd chosen not to share with Florence the over-heard conversation between Giles and Rufus, or Cecily's words about Florence and Giles being house-hoggers. She hadn't mentioned the bruise she'd detected around Ophelia's eye either. She wanted a bit more time to think on her own before she heightened her cousin's already sky-rocketing levels of anxi-ety. To accuse the wrong person would be awful, and may very well produce more problems than answers. And the awful fact was that she needed to include Florence in her mental list of possible suspects. Yes, she needed time to mull things over, decide the best way forward. She stood up.

'Let's go back to the house,' she said. 'I'm rather looking forward to meeting this woman.'

8

Digby watched as Ophelia rinsed the soles of Sam's wellies under the tap in the outhouse. Sam was outside somewhere, playing on the lawn.

'You're wasting water,' he said, reaching over to turn the tap off.

'I haven't finished yet, Digby.' Ophelia turned the tap on. 'Don't turn it off yet, there's still a lot of mud on them.'

Digby reached over and turned the tap off again.

'You're not cleaning them in the most efficient way, Ophelia,' he said, his mouth a sneer. 'You never learn, do you? If I was doing it the boots would be clean by now.'

An anger so long suppressed welled up with ferocity inside Ophelia. She turned the tap back on and continued scrubbing the soul of the wellington boot, saying nothing.

Digby stepped closer to her, she could feel his acid breath on her neck. He reached forward and turned the tap off again.

'Just leave me alone.' Ophelia turned, her voice louder than she usually dared. 'I'm trying to help Sam, Digby, by cleaning his boots. It might help you, too, because then they will be ready if you want to take him out again tomorrow. Leave me to get on with it, please.'

Digby picked up the heavy iron bucket that stood on the sink's counter and brought it crashing down on to the back of Ophelia's right hand that was still in the sink next to the wellie, putting all his force into the action. She screamed, sharp pain shooting through the bones in her hand and up her arm.

'Shut up,' he hissed. 'It was your fault I did that. You shouldn't have answered me back, should you? Don't cry, it's pathetic. You know how it annoys me when you cry.'

'My hand.' Ophelia held it in front of her, tears streaming down her face. 'It really hurts, Digby.'

'Like I said, it was your fault that happened.' A vein was bulging at the side of Digby's forehead. 'I wouldn't have done it if you hadn't spoken to me so rudely.'

Ophelia turned away from him. Her thoughts were splintering, fragmenting amid the shattering pain. She couldn't go on like this for much longer, she knew. But then she had to, for Sam. Digby had made it quite clear that if she ever left he would take Sam with him and she'd never see the boy again.

Neither of them saw the eyes staring at them through the crack in the door.

9

Lucie stared at her husband. She was sitting on their bed in the brown room, as Florence called it. She was finding the heavy old furniture packed in to the space as oppressing as the current conversation.

'No, we can't just "go back home",' she said, sighing. 'I want to, too, Neil. I hate being here, it's a bloody nightmare. Araminta's an arch bitch, Rufus is as drunk as she is most of the time, Coco's a psycho and Wilfred's just weird. Mummy's as cold as ever and Daddy seems to have emotionally cut himself off from everyone. Sister Veronica seems all right but she keeps looking at me in a funny way, and Magnus is just a lost cause. Maud's just boring. I barely know Digby and Ophelia, haven't seen them for ages. But Uncle Giles has just died and poor Aunt Florence is in bits. We can't just leave now, I have to make sure she's okay. And besides...' Lucie played with the duvet she was sitting on. 'We came here to discuss something with her, didn't we?'

Neil's expression had shifted from hopeful back to resigned while she was talking.

'I hate it here,' he said in a low voice. 'It's uncomfortable. I never feel welcome, and your mother blatantly dislikes me. And the boys don't enjoy it either. They're away from everything they love, their computer games and their friends.'

'I know that.' Lucie's voice was rising. 'But what do you want me to do, Neil? We can't even pay our bills at the moment, and I had to take out a loan to buy the boys some Christmas presents. Just wait a bit, and when the time's right I'll have a chat with Aunt Florence.'

'If you weren't doing that PhD...' Neil muttered, turning away.

'If I wasn't studying for this doctorate, yes, I'd still have my job at the council,' Lucie said, half-shouting now. 'But I'm not just doing this for me, Neil. I'm doing it for *us*, and the boys. I want to do something meaningful with my life, not just push paper around and enter meaningless data forever. In just over a year I'll have finished, and I'll be qualified to get a much better job then. We just have to hang on for a bit longer. Can't you see that?'

'It's just taking so long.' Neil turned back, a muscle throbbing in his jaw. 'I'm doing all the extra shifts I can at the warehouse, Luce. I'm exhausted, I can't keep that amount of overtime up much longer. And most of all, I – I don't want this to affect our marriage. But we've been financially fucked for ages now, since you left your job in fact. Can't you see how it's affecting our relationship? All the stress? All the trying to make ends meet?'

Hot tears welled up in Lucie's eyes. She blinked fast.

'Yes. I know,' she said. 'You're right, Neil, and I'm so sorry it's put such a burden on you. I just need your support for a bit longer. This means so much to me. Please?'

She stared at her husband, his face tight with stress. He'd lost weight over the last few months, his clothes were getting baggier on him. And all because of the anxiety he felt trying to earn enough so that she could finish her studies into domestic abuse. It was an issue she'd felt passionately about, ever since her friend Melody had been mercilessly beaten up by her partner. Lucie had supported Melody as much as she could, found the domestic abuse helpline details for her, helped her move house to a safe place her violent partner didn't know about, seen the effect the whole thing had had on Melody's two young children. Lucie had always felt huge compassion for the underdogs in life, the vulnerable and oppressed, she couldn't help it. She sometimes thought she'd been born with too many emotions to cope with. 'Too sensitive', her sister Araminta always called her. Well, now she wanted to use her empathy to help vulnerable women and men. She felt so strongly about finishing her PhD that she was prepared to stand up to her husband about it. But the last thing she wanted was for it to affect their relationship, to make their lives unbearable.

Ophelia concerned her. What the hell was all that about that drip Digby choosing her clothes, and slagging her off to Sam? Lucie knew the signs, especially after supporting Melody for so long. Ophelia was in a bad situation, she could just tell that from the brief time they'd spent together. She hadn't seen her cousin for years, of course, it wasn't like the extended family met up regularly or anything. They weren't the type, too bloody selfish. And she actively avoided spending time with her sister, snooty cow that she was.

It was funny, in a sad sort of way, Lucie reflected, because she'd always envied Ophelia, who seemed to have all the looks and charm a girl could want. They didn't see very much of each other, the last time they'd met up was before Sam was born. She'd seemed quiet then, more subdued than she remembered her, but no warning signs, no hint that anything was wrong. Yet here Ophelia was a few years later, seemingly and unfathomably under the control of Digby. She wanted to talk to her cousin about it, get her to open up and share whatever was going on, but she also knew that going in too heavy-handed would most likely make Ophelia back away and tell her nothing. Lucie felt lucky to have the husband she did. Of course, they'd had their arguments and bad times, they were in the middle of one now. But he was a good person, so kind and thoughtful. She never wanted to lose him.

'Listen, Neil,' she said to his back view. 'I'll talk to Aunt Florence soon, I promise. Let's just stay a few more days until I find the right moment, okay?'

'Fine,' Neil said, without looking at her. 'Whatever. I'm going to find the boys.'

Lucie stared at the bedroom door as it swung closed after his departure. This was bad; she hadn't seen him this down for, well, as long as she could remember. Right. She must talk to Auntie Florence, even if this was the most horrendous and awkward time to do so. But how on earth would she go about asking for money when her aunt's husband had just died?

10

Romilly turned out to be very different from whatever Sister Veronica had been expecting. An incredibly tall, chubby woman, she wore her mousy brown hair scraped back in a low ponytail, and spoke to everyone in a soft voice. She wore a perpetual look of disappointment on her fleshy face and Sister Veronica felt thwarted that the woman standing at the kitchen counter in front of her was not the fiery energy ball she'd been imagining. Could this dowdy person really be responsible for Magnus' defeated persona? It was hard to imagine how.

'Oh, Wilfred, are you making a mess again?' Romilly's voice was softly accusing. 'You always make more work for people, don't you? Just like your father. It's a very selfish habit. I'm always mindful of everyone. I was hoping you might notice one day and take heed.'

'Oh, Romilly, are you being passive aggressive again?' Wilfred mimicked his mother's tone, not looking up from his dinosaur craft extravaganza.

'That's a hurtful thing to say.' Romilly's mouth turned down at the corners. 'I don't even know what passive aggressive means. It's outright anger I can't stand. Doesn't hurt to be polite to people, I always think. Don't you get any exercise anymore, Wilfred? Do you just stay in the house like this day after day?'

'Yes, I've developed an allergy to sunlight,' Wilfred said. 'If the rays touch my bare skin I turn to dust. Plus, I'm on the way to becoming a hermit. It's what I want to be when I grow up. I plan to never leave the house for years.'

'Now.' Florence bustled between them, going over to switch the kettle on. 'Wilfred, don't be rude to your mother, and stop being silly. Hello, Romilly, here again, I see. I'm not sure you've heard but Giles passed away unexpectedly yesterday, so today is very hard for us here. I'm sure you won't be staying for long, perhaps just a quick tea?'

'I'm sorry to hear that, of course, but you seem to be trying to get rid of me as soon as I've arrived, Florence. As usual.' Romilly gave a small, long-suffering smile. 'Yes, I'll have a tea, thank you.' She settled herself on a bar stool at the counter. 'Although I'm never wanted here.'

Sister Veronica watched the woman with interest as delicious smells wafted up from the oven. Her remarks were so full of 'victim' it was fascinating. Mrs Hardman must be around somewhere but she still hadn't met the elusive housekeeper yet. She suspected Wilfred's diagnosis of passive-aggressiveness regarding his mother was correct. She'd only been with Romilly for a minute and already wanted to shake the woman. She had seen a different side to the boy since his mother had arrived. Up until now he'd seemed calm; detached but centred. Now there was a quiet anger exuding from him, and it was uncomfortable to watch his bad manners, however provoked they were.

'V, would you like one too?' Florence said over her shoulder.

'Yes please.' Sister Veronica let her eyes drop to Wilfred's decorations. He hadn't done much since she'd last seen them, she noticed. Perhaps he was a slow worker. Or maybe...

'Is Magnus around?' Romilly said. 'I've been trying to get

hold of him, but he never answers my texts. And I always answer people straight away. It's very rude of him.'

'Is there something desperately important you need to see my son about?' Sister Veronica detected an edge of rage in Florence's voice. 'He's just lost his father and I think he should be left alone for a few days, Romilly, to come to terms with it.'

'So that's this week's reason to try and keep me away from Magnus.' Romilly sniffed, reaching out to take the hot mug Florence was thrusting at her.

'It's the truth.' Florence's voice was getting louder. She picked up a tea towel to mop up some spilt water. 'It's not a bloody excuse.'

Sister Veronica stood up, walking over to her cousin.

'I'll take care of this, Flo,' she said in a low voice. 'You go and have a lie down.'

Florence nodded, throwing the tea towel down with force on to the counter before exiting the kitchen.

Sister Veronica made her own tea, generously heaping two sugars into it, suspecting she may need the energy, before rifling through the cupboards and retrieving an old packet of custard cream biscuits. She threw them on the counter in front of Romilly, and steadied herself on a bar stool opposite her, introducing herself and explaining her family connection to Florence.

'Oh yes, Magnus said there was a nun in the family.' Romilly regarded the packet of custard creams, a look of disdain briefly replacing her habitual disappointment. Wilfred reached across her and helped himself to three. Sister Veronica retrieved two for herself. 'Which is a surprise,' Romilly went on. 'As Magnus never tells me anything usually.'

'Well, you're divorced,' Wilfred said, turning to his mother. 'That's probably why he doesn't talk to you much. Goes with the territory, Romilly.'

'Don't call me that.' Romilly's mouth turned down slightly at the edges. 'It's rude. Call me mum or mummy, or even mother. Not Romilly.'

'Okay, Romilly.' Wilfred pushed his glasses up his nose before turning back to the vicious-looking creature he was working on, adding extra droplets of blood around the mouth.

Romilly sighed.

'They're all so horrible to me, Sister. All the time. I don't know what I've done to deserve it, I'm a good person, and I do my best by everyone.' Her brow furrowed. 'I'm so nice to this family but I feel like they throw it back at me, and the worst thing is that Wilfred is copying them now.'

'Yet the children don't live with you?' Sister Veronica said. 'Any reason for that?'

'Dad is less annoying,' Wilfred said, wiping a crumb from his mouth. 'Romilly makes us feel bad about everything all the time.'

'No I don't, what a horrid thing to say.' Romilly picked up her mug. 'You've always had the Beresford insolence, haven't you, Wilfred? Honestly, I think you're a lost cause, there's no hope for you, not coming from the line you do.'

'Yep.' Wilfred nodded, not looking up. 'You've got it right, absolutely. I'm a lost cause.'

'You'll turn out like your grandfather Giles, if you're not careful,' Romilly said, taking a sip of tea.

'What, dead?' Wilfred said.

'No, of course not, I didn't mean that.' Romilly's voice was soft, hurt. 'What a mean thing to say, trying to make it out like I would talk ill of the dead. I meant dislikeable. Not many people liked Giles.'

'You just spoke ill of my dead grandfather.' Wilfred's shading of his current dinosaur was getting darker and darker, Sister Veronica noticed.

'Why don't you go and get some fresh air, Wilfred,' she said. 'You've been in the kitchen for a long time now. Perhaps it's time for a break? Go on, spend a few minutes in the garden, you look like you need some fresh air.'

'Fine.' He put his pencil down, stood up, and walked out of the back door without a backward glance at his mother.

'So you think that not many people liked Giles?' Sister Veronica decided to push for information while she had the chance.

'The man was a bully.' Romilly sniffed. 'I'm not one to speak badly of anyone, but the simple fact is that Giles was an egotistical tyrant who treated his workforce very unfairly. Always firing people for no reason, or taking away their bonuses. Must have paid himself a handsome wage though, I mean just look around. Not a cheap house to keep and they've just had a new kitchen fitted.'

Sister Veronica looked around. Yes, she supposed it all did look new and shiny, in a rustic style sort of way. It was a large space, with two ovens – she suspected one was an Aga – long polished sideboards and country-style cupboard doors. There was an island in the centre, surrounded by the bar stools they were sitting on. The thing is she never really noticed new things until someone pointed them out, she wasn't that interested in them. But people, on the other hand, were a different matter. Her interest and fascination most definitely lay in them, she loved trying to understand all sorts, all types of personalities, puzzling out what made them tick. And more to the point, working out the motives behind people's words and actions.

'How do you know how Giles treated his workers? Did you do some work for him?' she said, turning back to Romilly.

'No, I'd never do that.' Romilly gave a bitter chuckle. 'It would be too hellish. Giles gave my brother a job for a few months, before he fired him. His excuse for letting him go was that Steven was always late in the mornings, and therefore was unreliable. But he was only a few minutes behind schedule a couple of times. I mean, really. What kind of reason is that to let someone go?'

'Was that the only reason?' Sister Veronica said, picking up a custard cream.

Romilly shifted, a look of discomfort crossing her face.

'Yes,' she said, after a pause. 'That was the only reason. Magnus couldn't even hack his own father's domineering manner. He tried to work for the old bastard several times but in the end something happened and he got signed off with stress. He'd never tell me exactly what had gone on, just that he'd had enough and was never going back.'

'Is that so?' Sister Veronica said through a mouthful of crumbs. 'Now, that's very interesting.'

'Magnus finds life very stressful in general,' Romilly said. 'I had to do everything when we were together, earn the money, pay the rent and the bills. Not that he ever thanked me for it.'

'What do you do?' Sister Veronica said. 'Workwise, I mean.'

'I'm a civil parking enforcement officer,' Romilly said.

Sister Veronica thought for a moment.

'Oh, do you mean you put parking tickets on car windscreens?' she said.

'There's a lot more to it than that,' Romilly said, sniffing. 'Although most people don't realise. I'm on my feet all day. No one is ever nice to me at work either.'

'No, I don't expect they are,' Sister Veronica said absentmindedly. Her brain was full of whirling thoughts, each presenting different people's motives to her. So Magnus was signed off with stress because something had happened when he was working at his father's fish finger business, Beresford's Breaded Wonders. Romilly had clearly never liked Giles, and she'd already overheard Rufus and Cecily's reasons for having issues with the man. What about Lucie and Neil? And did she need to include the children in her investigation? And Maud? Maud was Giles' blood relative, surely there wouldn't be any reason to include her. And, of course, there was Ophelia and Digby to think about. Sam, being four, could reasonably be excluded from suspicion. She hated to think of this, but what about Florence? The man must have been very difficult to live with, perhaps Florence had just had enough? And then there were the awful letters Florence had told her about. Could the person behind them have killed Giles? Goodness gracious, what a family. Where was the love in this household? Why was everyone so disparaging of each other?

Footsteps came running up the passage towards the kitchen.

'Oh my God,' Coco shouted as she entered. 'Oh my *God*, the police are here. They must have found out about Daddy.'

'What do you mean, Coco?' Sister Veronica asked quickly, standing up. 'What's happened to your father?'

'He takes drugs.' Coco's voice became a wail. 'He's a drug addict. I caught him smoking a spliff this morning, I can't believe it. What kind of example is he setting to me?'

'Is he doing that again?' Romilly rolled her eyes. 'Cannabis has always been his weakness.'

'You knew?' Coco shouted. 'Why didn't you tell me?'

'I think the police are probably here because of Giles,' Sister Veronica said as she walked past Coco and Romilly towards the door. 'Not Magnus. Shall we all calm down and go and find out?'

11

Ophelia sat on the side of Sam's bed. Digby had taken the boy out again without telling her. She had no idea where they were, or when they would be back. An aching emptiness was eating up her insides. She felt like Sam was slipping away from her, after everything she'd endured to keep him and her together. When the fear surrounding every aspect of Digby's treatment of her receded, she detected a hatred of him inside her. Not just a hatred, but an all-consuming loathing. No, she couldn't give in to it, he would use it against her. Look at what had happened when she was washing Sam's wellies.

She raised her aching hand. A purple-and-blue bruise was starting to come to life across the top of it. She would have to use thick foundation on it, like she did with the bruise on her eye. She hoped no one would notice, she didn't think they had so far. For a while she'd thought the old nun might have spotted something, the way she was looking at her. But she'd never said anything so Ophelia had come to the conclusion that Sister Veronica must look at everyone in that strange, intense way she had.

Loneliness was an all-pervasive experience. To be so alone,

yet among family, was even worse. Not that they were really her family, not her blood relatives at any rate. Her father Tarquin had been getting on in years when he and her mother had adopted her. They hadn't told her much about her birth parents, just that they hadn't been in a position to look after a baby. She didn't even know their names. She'd always felt like an outsider, never like a true part of the family. Oh, her mother and father had been kind enough, in a distant, formal way, and she'd never wanted for anything. Been left a tidy inheritance when they'd passed, within two years of each other, that Digby had enjoyed slowly taking over and controlling. He said she was bad with money. But it was her money. And she wasn't bad with it, just bought things that were needed. Well, she used to, before she was given a certain amount a month, and a pocket book to write down all her spending in so he could rake over it every evening and question her about each item.

'You *bought* a coffee?' he'd ask. 'When we have coffee here at home?'

'Yes, Digby,' she'd reply. 'I was meeting Lisa in a café. You can't bring your own coffee into cafés.'

'It's a waste of money,' he'd say. 'Invite Lisa here. I don't want you buying any more drinks, they are a luxury you can do without.'

Every inch of her life was now controlled by her husband. And the worse thing was, she couldn't tell anyone because he'd take Sam away from her. He threatened it enough. Lucie seemed nice, she hadn't seen her for years, and Ophelia felt compelled to take her into her confidence and explain what was going on. Of course it wasn't normal that Digby bought all her clothes, or encouraged Sam to put her down, or controlled her money. But because of what she'd done he now had her in this suffocating bind that she couldn't escape, because the price of freedom meant losing the person she loved most in the world, her little boy, and she just wasn't prepared to do that. And because Digby had now transferred what was left of her inheritance into his own private bank account, she had no means to leave him in secret, and take Sam with her. She was stuck, trapped.

Ophelia had thought about taking her own life more than once. She fantasised about suicide, because it gave her a sense of peace, the thought of all the pain going away. But in reality she could never do it to Sam. It made her laugh how people said she was pretty, how they thought she had it made. If only they knew the truth.

There was a fuss going on downstairs in the hall, she could hear raised voices, and Coco screaming about something. But she had no interest in it, she just wanted Sam to come back. She lay down on his bed and breathed his pillow, his familiar smell making her heart ache. As the voices downstairs grew louder, Ophelia shut her eyes. A single tear rolled down her cheek.

12

'What in Great Saints in Heaven is going on here?' Sister Veronica arrived in the entrance hall, and surveyed the scene, Florence arriving from wherever she'd been resting seconds later. Her gaze took in Araminta, who seemed to have just finished falling down the stairs and was now in a heap at the bottom, the reek of alcohol oozing from her like a bad perfume. *That was quick work*, she thought. *It can't have been an hour since I last saw her and now she's comatose with liquor.* She studied the woman for a moment, trying to work out whether any serious injury had been sustained. *No*, she concluded. *I don't think so. Just a bad drunken concussion.* She observed the two police officers – one in plain clothes and one in uniform – standing just inside the door, also staring at the tableau in front of them. She couldn't help but listen to Coco's shrieks, which seemed to mainly be about just having watched Auntie Araminta tumble down the stairs from the first floor to the ground. She saw Wilfred's amused face, Romilly's triumphant one, Rufus' blotchy countenance as he knelt down beside his wife, and Lucie coming down the stairs, shock creeping into her eyes. Maud had finally risen, perhaps nudged from her room by the noise. There was a look of gentle concern on her plump face as she watched the goings-on from her stance next to the Christmas tree.

'Oh for God's sake,' Florence muttered in her ear. 'This is all we bloody need.'

'What's all the racket about?' Cecily bustled in from the direction of the living room. 'Barnaby and I have been trying to read the papers in peace, but... Oh.' She stopped as she caught sight of her eldest daughter in a drunken sprawl on the floor. 'Araminta. Get up this instant and stop making such a fool out of yourself.'

'I don't think she can,' Rufus said, looking round, his voice a slur. 'She seems to have knocked herself out. Minty and I had a bit of a drinky earlier than usual today. She finished off a whole bottle of whisky – couldn't get the thing out of her hands, she was a woman possessed, chugged the whole lot. Then the silly mare tripped at the top of the stairs and fell all the way down. I think she was on the hunt for more booze. Sorry and all that, everybody. Don't worry too much, she's done it before and she's always fine after a few minutes.'

'Oh my God, she's going to die,' Coco screamed. 'She's not moving.'

'I'm calling an ambulance,' one of the police officers said. She turned and began talking into her radio.

'Florence Beresford?' the other officer said, looking around at the various faces before him.

'Yes, that's me,' Florence said, stepping forward.

'Ah, hello. I'm Detective Inspector Ahuja. Is there somewhere we can go to talk in private?'

'Yes, of course.' Florence, grey-faced, ushered the police officer quickly away. The other officer, having finished with her radio, introduced herself as PC Johnson.

'What's been going on here then?' she said.

'We've all been very shocked by poor Giles' death,' Cecily

said, taking a few steps around the prone body of her daughter. 'I suppose we're all dealing with it in our different ways. Araminta's coping mechanism seems to be alcohol.'

'She's always bloody drunk, Mummy,' Lucie said, walking down the stairs. 'Let's not make excuses. It doesn't matter what day it is, or who died, she and Rufus just drink their lives away. Don't you?' She turned towards her brother-in-law. 'She never used to do that before she met you, Rufus. Oh, she's always been a bitch, but never such a hammered one.'

'Now wait a minute.' Rufus stood up, staggering from one foot to the other. Sister Veronica could smell the sour stench of alcohol on him from where she stood a few feet away. 'I know Minty and I aren't exactly angels, but neither are you, Luce. Look at the way you're still insisting on carrying on with your pointless PhD when poor Neil is working his fingers to the bone trying to cover all your expenses. I might enjoy the odd glass of wine–' Lucie snorted. 'But I'm not far gone enough not to recognise stress in a man when I see it. Don't you think it's selfish of you to put him in that position?'

'Firstly,' – Lucie reached the bottom of the stairs, stepped over her sister, and went right up to Rufus – 'my PhD isn't pointless, thank you very much. And secondly, you have no idea what's going on in my marriage, so keep your drunken ramblings to yourself.'

Sister Veronica heard footsteps approaching the open front door. It was Neil, Nathan and Ryan, covered in mud, rosy-cheeked and laughing. Neil stopped when he saw the carnage going on in the hall, and put his arm out to stop his sons from entering. The smile left his face, and his darkening eyes met his wife's.

'Right boys,' he said, turning, a curt tone to his voice. 'I think we'll go back out into the garden and carry on with practising our passes and tackles. Seems a bit too crowded for us in here.'

Sister Veronica observed Lucie's downcast gaze as the three of them turned and left. *Hmm, maybe Rufus is right*, she thought. *Perhaps all is not well with their marriage. That's a shame, they do seem to suit each other well.*

She heard a door open and close down the corridor that led to the dining room. A small, thin, perfectly contained-looking woman appeared, wearing a white apron. Her greying hair was pulled away from her long, sallow face in a tight bun. Sister Veronica stared at her in surprise. Who on earth was this person, suddenly appearing in the heart of the house? It only took a second for her to work it out.

'Ah, Mrs Hardman.' Barnaby shuffled out of the living room, his mop of white hair as dishevelled as ever. He didn't even look at his daughter on the floor, or at the police officer, instead keeping a slow but steady beeline for the housekeeper. 'Something smells nice?' He looked at the old grandfather clock to his right. 'Ah, half past one. Must be lunchtime.'

Indeed, Sister Veronica agreed silently. Delicious smells of hot food abounded in the hall, seeming somewhat incongruous when the unpleasantness of the current situation was considered. It was strange how those contrasts often happened in life, she thought. The dark running concurrently with the light, the duality of existence always being reminded to us, especially in times of trouble. Perhaps it was the universe's way of pointing out to humans just how ridiculous we make life sometimes, when actually it could be so much better if we made slightly different choices.

'That's right,' Mrs Hardman said quietly, a gentle lilt of something – Irish? – in her accent. 'In fact, I just came to tell you all that lunch is ready to be served.' She turned and walked back down the corridor, Barnaby trailing behind her like a lapdog. Maud gave a smile and followed suit; the idea of her next meal obviously being more entertaining than the current drama. Wilfred shrugged and went too.

'Where's Daddy?' Coco said, looking around. She opened her mouth. 'Daddy!' she screamed.

'Oh shut up,' Lucie said, a fierceness in her voice. 'Just go and find him quietly, there's a good girl.'

For a moment, Sister Veronica thought Coco was going to answer her aunt back. But for once, she contented herself with stomping off without saying anything. Perhaps the presence of PC Johnson had deterred a full-blown outburst, Sister Veronica thought.

'Honestly,' Lucie muttered. 'That girl behaves more like she's seven than seventeen.' Sister Veronica smiled in what she hoped was a sympathetic manner. *But why?* she wondered. *What is causing Coco to act like that? Does she want attention? She and her mother barely glanced at each other in the few moments they were together. Honestly, this family – my family – is so very strange.*

'Araminta's always gone over the top, hasn't she?' Romilly looked round, a smirk playing at the corners of her mouth. 'I don't think I've seen her sober for years. Such a shame for her, to have so little self-control, and such poor disregard for her own body.'

Lucie shot her a poisonous look, but said nothing. PC Johnson turned and stared down the driveway, perhaps wondering when the ambulance would come so she could get out of this madhouse. Rufus didn't appear to have heard. He'd wobbled back down into a crouching position and was staring at his wife's face. It was Cecily who turned to take up the bait.

'Sorry, Romilly, but why exactly are you here?' Her thin voice was harsh. She looked Romilly up and down. 'Come to see your children, perhaps? You don't seem to be paying much attention to them. Or come to browbeat your ex-husband as per usual?'

Well, to be fair she doesn't seem to be paying much attention to her unconscious daughter either, Sister Veronica thought. *But perhaps this is Cecily's way of defending her family, by attacking any critics.*

'I have a right to be here,' Romilly said in a little voice that contrasted so glaringly with her big size.

'No, Romilly, you don't,' Cecily said. '*I* have a right to be here, more right than most, in fact. But you most certainly don't belong here.'

'Magnus stole my children,' Romilly said.

'*No*, he *didn't*.' Cecily took a step forward, her voice soft. 'You know as well as I do that both Coco and Wilfred chose to live here with Magnus, rather than go back to live with you. Perhaps the question you should be asking yourself is why that is. Now, if I'm not mistaken, Romilly, it's time for you to leave. The ambulance will be here for Araminta soon, and above all else, it's lunchtime, and Mrs Hardman won't have made enough for you.'

'See, Sister?' Romilly said as she walked past, drawing herself up to her full towering height. 'I told you they were all horrid to me here. And I never do anything to deserve it. You've all made it clear I'm not welcome. Again. I'll come and see Magnus and the children again soon. Maybe tomorrow.'

'No, *not* tomorrow, Romilly,' Cecily said, her voice firm. But Romilly exited through the front door without showing signs of having heard her.

A voice came crackling over PC Johnson's radio.

'Ah, the ambulance is just coming down the drive,' she said, looking up, a tinge of relief in her voice. 'Who's going to travel with Araminta to the hospital?'

Cecily and Rufus looked at one another, neither rushing to volunteer.

'I'll go, of course,' Rufus said after a brief pause, staggering to his feet again. 'Minty will be fine. This is a lot of fuss about nothing.'

'Certainly, if you'd rather go with her, that's all right by me.' Cecily gave a small smile. *Goodness gracious*, Sister Veronica thought. *If that was my daughter unconscious on the floor, nothing would stop me from being with her. What kind of warped love abounds in this family? It seems I was very lucky to have the parents I did. I got off lightly.*

Images of her mother and father, Rosalind and Albert, flashed through her mind. Her ruddy-faced mother was mad old Henrietta's younger sister, and while slightly eccentric – with traditional views about a woman's place in the home – Rosalind had been a loving and stable presence throughout her child-hood years. Her mother had married 'down', according to family legend, falling in love with a farmer's son when she was young. *Best thing for her*, Sister Veronica thought now, looking around. *She freed herself, and me, from all this. We didn't have much when I was a child, but the atmosphere at home certainly wasn't like it is at Chalfield Hall. In my house, it was much lighter, full of love. That's how it should be, if you ask me. Oh, we had our dark times, when the universe tested our resolve, but then everyone does, don't they? It's part of life. Every day isn't supposed to be hard though. Not like this. No, my childhood house wasn't constantly full of tension, secrets and conflict, and for that I'm grateful.*

A few minutes later, the softly groaning Araminta – her eyelids flickering – and Rufus, dishevelled and pale, were packed into the ambulance by the paramedics and trundled away. Something in Cecily's words had caught her peripheral attention, Sister Veronica reflected, as she made her way towards the dining room, leaving PC Johnson to wait patiently for the detective in the hall. *What had the woman said? Oh yes, 'I have a right to be here, more right than most, in fact.' Now why would she phrase her words like that? Why did she have more right than anyone else?*

13

After a hearty lunch of Mrs Hardman's home-made chicken pie and vegetables followed by an extraordinarily moist sponge cake slathered with warm custard – not quite as tasty as her favourite biscuits that shared the same flavour but a close second – Sister Veronica allowed herself a few moments of respite away from the melee. So much had happened in such a short space of time, she was feeling rather overwhelmed and in need of taking stock and going through everything. It was the day before Christmas Eve, for heaven's sake, not that it felt like it. She found that when she stopped to think about things – the awfulness of Giles' death, the terror at someone close to her potentially being a killer and the feeling that something else bad was going to happen – it calmed a bit, as though by thinking, she were doing something to help the situation. Florence had not yet reappeared after disappearing with DI Ahuja, and she hoped her cousin was well, and not being told anything too unpleasant, or being asked a lot of uncomfortably personal questions.

Settling herself into the most hidden bamboo chair in the conservatory – a big space that adjoined the living room – Sister Veronica stared out of the window at the bare trees lining the huge patch of lawn in front of the house. The sky was white, with a silvery pale-pink haze misting up behind the trees. She sniffed the air. Hmm, snow was on its way, if she wasn't mistaken. Good, there was something cosy about being snowed in, about battening down the hatches and drinking steaming hot chocolate while watching the unforgiving elements swirl outside. And it might give the family a much-needed diversion to concentrate on; little Sam – at least – would enjoy making a snowman.

Two figures were walking down the drive – due to their size difference it looked as though it was Digby and Sam. She'd wondered where they and Ophelia were at lunch, had presumed they'd all gone out for the day. Perhaps Digby would make a sandwich in the kitchen for both of them. The boy would be hungry now. And goodness knows where Magnus had got to, she hadn't seen him for ages. *Probably away with the fairies on cannabis, if Coco was to be believed, although I'm not sure she's fully accurate with the truth at all times*, she thought. *Still, it seems a strange thing for her to invent.*

Anyway, she thought, collecting herself. *Giles is dead, presumed murdered by this poison – what was it called? Oh yes, abrin. I must find out exactly what that is. Now, the thing is, there appears to be two people with possible motives who were visibly annoyed with Giles in front of me: Cecily and Rufus. There's always Barnaby as well, although his head seems to be away in some other far-off world most of the time. It's Cecily who's made remarks about wanting to live in the house, and has just said she deserves to be here more than most, which is strange. And it was Rufus who argued with Giles just before he died, accusing him of doing something bad, and that he was dishonest, and that he had to stop doing whatever it was. But what was it? Now that is the unanswerable question. At least for now. And Magnus was signed off with stress after working for Giles. Could whatever caused that be enough to make Magnus want to kill* his own father? Although arguably it could have been any one of us in this house who killed Giles, even Mrs Hardman. Well, I know it wasn't me, so that just leaves Cecily, Barnaby, Rufus, Araminta, Lucie, Neil, Maud, Magnus, Digby, Ophelia, and Florence – if we have to include all the adults. And Romilly must also be counted in, she's here often enough. Then, of course, a handful of children and teens. Would Coco, Wilfred, Ryan or Nathan have it in them? Sam can obviously be discounted. And there are the poison pen letters Florence told me about. I'm pretty sure it was these making her ill with worry before she found Giles. Are they connected to Giles' murder in some way? Who on earth could be sending them? And, on what I'm sure is a separate note, there is something very odd about Digby and Ophelia's relationship, and whatever it is concerns me very much. But they are both very closed. I think it's going to be hard work trying to get anything out of her. I'm almost certain he won't open up to me. And, of course, after today's debacle, I'm pretty sure Araminta and Rufus are raging alcoholics. Drinking like that before lunch, they should be ashamed of themselves. A whole bottle of whisky too. Honestly, the spectacle was too much.

She sat up, hearing the living-room door open and close. Dash, she'd been hoping for a bit of peace, but that was almost impossible to find in this house. Someone was chatting away merrily, but there was only one voice, not two. Who was it? Oh, Coco. She sounded infinitely happier than usual.

Trying to be as covert as possible, Sister Veronica peeked round the side of the chair until she could see into the living room. Coco was holding her phone about a foot away from her face, and was smiling, posing and chatting away in front of the screen. She looked different, no scowl to be seen, her eyes lit up in a positively radiant way, making her look rather beautiful. Clearly, she'd given up on her quest to find Magnus, having found something more interesting to do. The girl's quick changes in mood were startling; she could go from hysterical to relatively calm in seconds, then back to frenzied again, a phenomenon Sister Veronica had witnessed several times since arriving in Northamptonshire. Every now and again she saw Coco pause; someone seemed to be talking back to her on the phone, but she couldn't hear what they were saying. She frowned. The girl was hardly wearing any clothes, just a tiny vest-like thing and miniscule shorts. Hardly suitable, especially considering the cold weather. Then the door opened and Wilfred walked in, crashing it shut behind him.

'Trying to impress all your lovers again?' He snorted, walking past his sister, who put her arm out and punched him.

'I'm doing a live on Instagram for my fans,' Coco said. 'I've got 5,308 followers now. Go away, Wilfred.' But she said it in a normal voice, not screeching or berating him. *Hmm, so she can switch on the charm when she wants*, Sister Veronica mused, turning back round to gaze out of the window. *That girl really is a puzzle to me. And what on earth is a live on Instagram?*

'Ah, there you are.' Wilfred arrived in the conservatory, throwing himself into a bamboo chair next to Sister Veronica's, staring at her intently. 'I've been looking for you.'

'Have you indeed?' Sister Veronica swivelled round to face him. 'What can I do for you, my boy?' *Goodbye peace and quiet*, she thought. *I hope he doesn't want to tell me anything else about dinosaurs, I don't think I can cope with any more of that.*

'I've found out what abrin is,' Wilfred said. 'I heard what you and Aunt Florence were saying in the garden. It sounded serious, so I've been researching it on my laptop.'

'So it *was* you spying on us.' Sister Veronica's eyebrows went up. 'I suspected as much when I saw how little art you'd done in my absence. Honestly, Wilfred, that's an incredibly rude and underhand thing to do. If I catch you sneaking around like that again, I'm going to tell Florence and your father.'

'Yes, all right,' Wilfred said, not looking at all apologetic. 'I knew you'd be cross. But I'm in training, I have to practise undercover operations. I'm going to be in MI6 when I'm older, you know, work for the intelligence service. I've got the brains for it.'

'And I see that modesty is your best quality,' Sister Veronica said. She shook her head, a frown taking over her face. 'Yes, I *am* cross, Wilfred. Your aunt and I were having a private conversation. You really must respect other people's boundaries.' At least it reduced the threat to her and Florence, she thought, if it was only Wilfred who had overheard what they were discussing.

'That's not all I found out in the garden.' Wilfred tried to look sly.

'What do you mean?' Sister Veronica's voice was sharp.

'When I left you and Aunt Florence I went the long way back to the kitchen. I heard voices in the outhouse so I peeped through the door to see who it was. It was Ophelia and Digby and they were having some sort of row. Digby picked up that old rusty bucket that's in there and smashed it onto Ophelia's hand. It looked like it really hurt her. He's a brute, I've never liked him. I don't know what she sees in him to be honest.'

Sister Veronica suddenly looked thoughtful.

'Is that so?' she said. 'No, you're right, Wilfred, Digby shouldn't be treating Ophelia like that, it's awful. Leave that piece of information with me, don't tell anyone else, okay? I have an idea about what to do. Right, let's hear it then. What have you found out about abrin?'

'Well,' Wilfred said, pushing his ever-slipping glasses up his nose. 'According to Google, abrin is a natural poison that's found in plants like rosary pea and the castor bean plant. The seeds in the berries of rosary pea are very poisonous and can definitely kill someone if they swallow them. I've just been having a look round the garden and in the greenhouse and there's a plant there that I think might match the description.'

'I see,' Sister Veronica said. 'So if what you're saying is correct, and the plant in the garden is rosary pea and contains abrin, the most likely scenario is that your grandfather either purposefully ate the berries, or someone tricked him into doing so. It just seems so strange, don't you think? That Giles would choose to eat them, or that he would be persuaded to do so?'

'I don't think he would eat them on purpose.' Wilfred scratched his forehead. 'I mean, why would Papa want to kill himself? He always seemed to enjoy life, he liked buying new cars and things, and he was saying how well his fish finger business was going at dinner that night wasn't he?'

'Yes, he was,' Sister Veronica said. 'But one thing I've learnt over the years, Wilfred, is that you never really know what's going on in someone's life. They can present an image of extreme happiness to the world, but actually be crumbling inside for some reason.'

'Well, you never know, but I still don't buy it,' Wilfred said. 'The other possibility, which I think is more likely, is that someone killed him.'

'Yes.' Sister Veronica looked at the boy, wondering if this thought upset him at all. Wilfred did tend to show a dissociation from his emotions, but this was his grandfather they were talking about, after all. 'Do you know if anyone had reason to dislike Giles, or if they would wish harm on him?'

'Oh, loads of people,' Wilfred said airily.

'What do you mean?' Sister Veronica's eyebrows raised.

'Well, mostly all the people he sacked at work,' Wilfred said. 'There was that big fuss when he fired Uncle Steven, Romilly's brother. Mum and Dad were still together at the time, and we were living down in the village. Papa said it was because Uncle Steven was always late to work, but I think there was more to it than that.'

'Why do you think that?' Sister Veronica said, feeling rather guilty for cross-questioning Wilfred about private family business. *But he's one of the most open members of the family*, she thought, trying to justify it to herself. *And I'm doing all this to help Florence.*

'Because of the big fuss that Romilly made,' Wilfred said. Sister Veronica marvelled at the boy's detachment from his own mother, but concluded that that was a conversation to have with him at another time. 'I mean, she's always berating people and making them feel bad, I think she nearly sent Dad insane with all that. But this was different, she was actually furious with Papa for what he did to Uncle Steven, and she and him and Dad were always whispering about it in the kitchen. I tried to listen to what they were saying but they were too clever for me to pick up on most of it. I did hear them saying something about going to a lawyer and trying to prosecute Papa though.'

'But you don't know what about?' Sister Veronica said.

'No,' Wilfred said. 'I don't think they ever went through with it, though, as Papa just seemed to carry on with his fish finger business as normal.'

Well, well, well. Sister Veronica's eyes went to the window, as she heard Nathan calling to Ryan to pass the ball. Those two were as outdoorsy and sporty as Wilfred was academic, she reflected. Polar opposites. Shame they didn't all play together really, Wilfred could do with a good runaround, he was so pale. So Romilly, her brother and Magnus were talking about prosecuting Giles. Perhaps whatever it was that was bothering them was linked to the situation Rufus had been angry with Giles about, just before his death. Could it be possible, she mused, that Wilfred's grandfather had been involved with something illegal that a few people stumbled on, and that in the end led to his downfall?

14

Cecily ran her finger along the back of the dresser in her and Barnaby's bedroom, the green room. Dust, she thought, looking at the gathering grey mound in disgust. And a lot of it. Honestly, Florence wasn't much of a housekeeper. Mrs Hardman was only employed to do the cooking and downstairs cleaning. The upstairs was Florence's responsibility, and she clearly wasn't up to the job. But then, she'd been letting herself go for years, hadn't she? The box of hair dye she knew her sister-in-law bought from the village pharmacy every three months made her look even more drab, with the beige glow it gave to her hair. Not that she'd used it for a while by the look of things, the grey stripe on top of her head was distinctly badgeresque. And her clothes – well. If you looked up the word 'dowdy' in a dictionary there would probably be a picture of Florence underneath it.

She turned back towards the room, and went over to shift the twin beds even further apart. She and Barnaby hadn't slept together under the same duvet for fourteen years, Cecily had made sure of that. It wasn't that Barnaby disgusted her exactly. He was a good old boy in his own way, had been dashingly handsome once, and was currently raking in a good pension now from his former law firm. But being physically close to him made her feel nauseous, and he hadn't objected when she'd first got rid of their king-sized bed and installed two twin beds in their home. Now the sleeping arrangement had become routine. Florence knew that they liked to have their own space, and always gave them the green room with the different beds. Cecily had told her sister-in-law in the beginning that it was because of Barnaby's snoring, and that if she was too close to him she could never fall asleep. That explanation seemed to satisfy most people, including her husband.

Giles, on the other hand, had been a different matter. Florence had never understood him like she – Cecily – had. She remembered how she'd first become close, very close, to Giles years ago when Magnus was just a teenager and Florence was having some self-consuming depressive episode. She'd always admired his flare and drive, finding his ego a turn-on where others seemed repelled by it. It had seemed natural for her and Giles to end up in bed together that night, after Florence had passed out on the sofa. Their affair had lasted for years, decades – always sporadic, always intense and passionate. But four years ago Giles seemed to have had an attack of conscience and had ended their relationship, saying he no longer wanted to deceive his wife. Probably found a younger model more like, Cecily thought, still ragingly bitter about his rejection.

Giles had never promised her anything other than love, but she knew she deserved to live at Chalfield Hall more than Florence, Magnus or anyone else. Hadn't it been her who'd spent hours listening to Giles' rage about his useless workforce, who had comforted him when things went wrong and who praised him when he'd turned them right again? Her sister-in-law didn't even like the house, she'd said several times over the years that the place was too big to run effectively. The mansion had naturally gone to Florence when mad old Henrietta had died, being the eldest of the old lady's three children – the order going Florence, Barnaby, then poor dead Tarquin – but Cecily knew it should have been her and Barnaby who'd got it, as she – Cecily – had actually wanted the house with a passion. But Barnaby had no real interest in trying to get hold of what should rightfully be theirs, he'd never been very materialistic, always happy to waft along in life letting other people take care of him. But she, on the other hand, yearned for the status of living at Chalfield Hall, of having a big house to host dinner parties in rather than their outdated cottage in the village. She'd mentally redecorated the place countless times, knew exactly what she would do with the garden – Florence was leaving it to look rather ramshackle these days – knew with precision who she would invite to her first dinner party there. Giles had always said the house would suit Cecily more than it suited Florence. Sometimes she'd fantasised about being Giles' wife and the two of them living there together. That would be a great partnership, and really give people something to talk about. But now there was no chance of that ever happening.

Cecily stared out of the window, at the boys practising rugby tackles on the front lawn. Common boys with common names, she thought. Lucie had married below her station, not like Araminta. Rufus came from a proper family, and had been schooled at Eton. She'd always approved of that match far more than Lucie and Neil's, and chose to overlook Araminta's excessive drinking in as much as was possible. She'd never felt particularly maternal towards either girl, had found their arrival in the world a hindrance to her social life. Barnaby seemed to love them in an absent sort of way, which was good, it made up for her innate lack of parental feeling. It had been him who'd taken them horse riding at the weekends when they were younger, and occasionally to the park or shopping in Northampton. Cecily was just glad that both girls were out of her hair now.

She wondered if Florence knew about her long-standing affair with Giles. She'd never shown any sign of doing so, was always irritatingly kind and polite when she and Barnaby arrived. Cecily snorted. What a doormat the woman was. No backbone in her at all. Perhaps, she mused, the best way forward would be to give Florence an almighty shock and tell her about the affair. Maybe that would make her want to finally move on, away from Chalfield Hall and all the shared memories there with Giles, allowing a free passage for Cecily and Barnaby to move in. Yes, Cecily thought. Maybe that was the way to go.

15

Araminta stared at the blue-and-white hospital curtains in front of her. Her head was pounding and her body ached. It had been quite a spectacular fall down the stairs, Rufus had told her, laughing, before visiting hours ended. Having her stomach pumped – again – had been as humiliating as usual. When would she learn to control her drinking? Urgh, why had she drunk all that whisky? She never wanted to be in this state again, feeling like an utter failure, a useless fat whale who did nothing but get smashed out of her mind on whatever alcohol was around.

But, oh, the sobriety was like a kick in the face. In one way she enjoyed sliding into the oblivion of drunkenness, feeling all her worries melting away, her inhibitions going, knowing she could say and do exactly what she wanted without caring at all. And the next morning, when the doubts crept in, she'd have a Bloody Mary – or whatever else was on hand – and top up the alcohol levels until any horrible thoughts went away again. But she knew her drinking wasn't healthy, and she hated the fact that she didn't seem to be able to stop doing it. It was a crutch, a bad coping mechanism. And the problem was, Rufus drank even more than she did, but he never seemed to experience the same side effects. Sure, he would slur his words and fall all over the place, but he had never actually hurt himself or gone unconscious like she had. For him, getting smashed went with the territory – all the other investment bankers she knew also drank like fish. It was just part of their lifestyle.

She'd felt that her existence was fairly pointless for a long time. If she was sober for too long, a gaping hole would expand inside her that was full of loss and an ache for something meaningful in her life. Up until now her quick remedy for that was to get extremely drunk as quickly as possible, and then the feelings and the gaping hole magically went away. But each time they reappeared, when she wasn't expecting them, they were worse, more expansive, deeper. Araminta knew she didn't actually like herself very much. And that was a soul-destroying thing to admit. She didn't like what she'd become, or how she and Rufus lived their lives.

A large part of this, she knew, stemmed from not being allowed to try for a baby. That had been Rufus' decision, all those years ago, and because she'd idolised him so much at the time, and never wanted to lose him, and above all valued the meagre pride her mother had shown when the two of them had married, she'd gone along with it. Neither of her parents had ever been particularly doting, although her father showed more signs of this than her mother. She'd often wondered what kind of mother she'd make, whether she'd treasure her child in a way her mother never could with Lucie and her. Araminta shook her head, remembering how she'd joined in when Rufus had talked about leechlike offspring who would ruin them and leave them no money. Laughed along with his derision of other people like her sister Lucie who were popping out babies right, left and centre. But deep down, Araminta had ached for a child. She thought she might be a better person if she were a parent and had someone else to love. She wasn't very good at liking herself, but a child would be a different matter. A beautiful innocent human being, who would bring out all the best sides of her, make her stop drinking, stop her from being shallow and facetious, and draw all the love in her to the surface.

It was true that Rufus and she lived a charmed life in many ways. They had travelled the world, had drunk their way around many countries, partied on yachts with elite crowds, and had never had to think about anyone except themselves. Until recently, well, they'd never had to worry much about money. But why, if that was all marvellous, did she feel so empty and awful when she was sober?

She sighed, turning her attention to the beeping blood pressure monitor to her right. The nurse would be back in soon, to take her vitals, and write them on the clipboard at the end of her bed. Then later today, or maybe tomorrow, she would be discharged, and have to go back to Chalfield Hall to face the looks that everyone would give her. And then, she would have to choose whether to stay sober and suffer the feelings of self-hatred and humiliation, or to yet again get drunk so she didn't have to feel anything at all. She knew what she *should* do, but doubted whether she had enough stamina to see it through. She'd tried many times, but there always came a point when her body started yearning for alcohol in such a primitive, strong way that was impossible not to give in to.

There was no point talking to Rufus about any of this. He would just laugh it off, tell her to stop turning into her square sister. Years ago, she'd tried to bring up the possibility of them having a child together, but it had been one of the rare occasions when he'd become angry with her.

'You said you never wanted children?' he'd spat. 'Why are you saying this now?'

So she'd dropped the subject and never brought it up again,

didn't dare to, as she couldn't bear the thought of him thinking badly of her. They were a team, her and Rufus, who got on well, and had lots of fun together. So why did she feel so miserable?

And then there was the secret they'd brought to Chalfield Hall. Absolutely no one knew about that. Even when she was drunk, Araminta knew she would never give it away. But it made a chill go through her just to think about it. Especially after what had happened with Giles.

16

Magnus was lying on the floor of the greenhouse, looking up at the transparent panels above him. *Spiders.* He chuckled. *Lots of them. Their webs are so pretty.*

He brought his fat spliff up to his lips and took a deep drag, holding the smoke in his lungs for a long time. Then he exhaled, allowing himself the pleasure of blowing a few smoke rings. Ah, now that was better. Just the very knowledge that his ex-wife Romilly had turned up was enough to send him scurrying into hiding. He'd heard the unmistakable squeal of her tyres on the gravel and had immediately removed himself from the family environment. Since rolling a generous, seven-Rizla paper joint, time had taken on a fluid, metaphysical quality. He had no idea how long he'd been in the greenhouse, or when Romilly had arrived, or whether she'd gone now. And it didn't matter, because nothing mattered. And it was wonderful.

His father, Giles, was dead. Magnus wondered if he should feel something about that. He currently didn't have any feelings at all. Perhaps they would come in time. He didn't even hate his dad at the moment, which was unusual, because he usually did. Maybe he'd forgiven him for what had happened, because he'd died? No, probably not. He was probably just too stoned to feel anything.

Magnus had a very faint feeling that he should probably know where his two children were, and have a rough idea about what they were doing. But he didn't, and right now that seemed absolutely fine to him. Anyway, there were enough adults around to keep an eye on them. Coco was probably having a hissy fit about something and Wilfred was probably reciting facts about fossils or dinosaurs to someone. He suspected that the fact he could no longer deal with his children – or with life in general – without being stoned, probably meant he was having some sort of breakdown. But right now, that didn't matter. Everything felt just fine.

He shut his eyes and enjoyed the floaty detached feeling that lifted his thoughts up and away. Nebulously, he wondered whether Romilly would have told anyone about what had happened with her brother Steven and his father, about the real reason his dad had fired the man. *I don't care if she has*, he thought to himself. He let out a big giggle. *I literally don't care.*

17

Sister Veronica accepted the steaming mug of tea Maud was holding out to her. Her eyes looked up and caught sight of the time; it had just turned half past three.

'Thank you,' she said. She was just about to attempt a conversation with the smiling woman, when the kitchen door opened.

'Ah, V,' Florence said. 'There you are. Would you like to come for a quick walk around the garden with me?' Her eyes seemed to be flashing some sort of message, Sister Veronica thought.

'Absolutely,' she said, taking a quick swig of tea before placing her mug on the counter. 'I was just thinking that I could do with some fresh air.'

Seconds later, the two of them were trudging along the path that led up through the lawn towards the orchard, the air around them noticeably chillier than it had been the previous day. Above them, a pale gold ray of sun managed to push its way through the thin white clouds.

'How did things go with the detective?' Sister Veronica asked, giving her cousin a sideways glance so she could assess how she was feeling. *Not too bad, by the looks of things.*

'Oh, fine, just as I expected really. Lots of questions about Giles, his business and personal life, whether there was anyone I knew about who would want to harm him. Well, I had to be honest and say that he did tend to rub a lot of people up the wrong way, but that I couldn't think of anyone who would actually want him dead.'

Yes, she looks a bit better now, Sister Veronica thought, as they slowed their pace under the bare branches of an apple tree. *Less pale, more together. A flush of colour in her cheeks. Perhaps talking it out with someone has been therapeutic. That sort of thing usually is.*

'Ah, as you said, those sorts of questions are to be expected,' she said, turning to Florence. 'Pretty standard. Did the detective say anything else, Flo?'

'Just that he wants to conduct interviews with everyone present at Chalfield the day Giles collapsed.' Florence frowned. 'He said we are all people of interest to the investigation, and that we might have noticed something that doesn't seem important to us, but that could tell the police a lot about what happened. He said he would be back tomorrow to start talking to people. Oh, V, it's the day before Christmas Eve today. But I don't feel festive at all, do you?'

'Not really,' Sister Veronica admitted. 'But I think we need to create as normal an atmosphere as possible for the children, Flo, don't you? We've neglected that, what with all the trouble that's been going on. It might help us all to listen to some carols or something. Do you have any Christmas music?'

'Yes, I'll find some when we go back to the house,' Florence said. 'V, have you had any more thoughts about what we should do? About who might have wanted Giles dead? It's making me shiver with fright to think I might be sharing my house with a murderer.'

'Yes, as a matter of fact, I have.' Sister Veronica looked around. There was no one about. 'And you are right to be scared,

Flo. I'm very afraid that we are all in danger, as long as whoever murdered Giles walks freely among us. Ah. Is that the greenhouse over there?' Florence nodded. 'Let's go over to it. If my information is correct, I may well be able to show you where the abrin that killed Giles came from.' *Not worth telling her about Wilfred at this point*, she thought. *Besides, the boy has a bright mind. I'd rather he keep telling me about what he's thinking as opposed to getting him into trouble at this stage.*

They traipsed through the long muddy grass towards the dirty-looking glass structure, green moss and lichen covering many of the panes.

'I really must take better care of the garden.' Florence looked around, despair on her face. 'If truth be told, I find this place overwhelming, V. It's too big. And the house has always seemed cold to me, do you know what I mean? Not in a chilly temperature kind of way, more in a spooky unsettling way. I've always thought I should feel lucky to have been given such a big place to live, especially when there are so many people in the world who have nothing. But to tell you the truth, I'd much rather live in a cosy cottage.'

'Some of the corridors here *are* rather dark.' Sister Veronica turned her head and looked at the back of the house. The big expanse of grey brick was imposing more than it was welcoming. Many of the upper windows were mean and small, and the decorative turrets put her in mind of a Transylvanian castle rather than an old English country home. She shivered. 'I never felt all that comfortable here as a child, if I'm honest.'

Arriving at the greenhouse, Florence took hold of the handle and swung the door open. A big whoosh of potent smoke assaulted Sister Veronica's nostrils, and she looked down to see where it was coming from.

'Magnus!' Florence said, one hand going to her face. 'Oh, not again.'

18

Digby and Sam were in the outhouse. Digby was taking ages cleaning their wellington boots on purpose, wanting to keep Sam away from his mother for as long as possible. He knew not seeing her son made Ophelia anxious, and she deserved to feel awful. It would help her learn not to go against his will.

'Do you remember what I said, Sam?' he asked the little boy, who was sitting on the side of the sink. 'What is Mummy?'

'Selfish,' said Sam.

'That's right,' Digby said, scrubbing miniscule bits of dirt from the largely clean sole of a boot. 'It might seem like she loves you, Sam, but actually she loves herself a little bit more. So that means she's selfish, and that she isn't a good mummy to you, doesn't it? I don't think she really loves you or me at all.'

'No,' Sam said, shaking his head.

'I want you to always remember that I love you the most, can you do that?' Digby looked over at his son.

'Yes,' Sam said.

'Good boy.' Digby turned the tap off. 'I'm a much better

parent to you than Mummy. She just ruins everything, doesn't she?'

'Yes,' Sam said. He wasn't smiling.

'Let's go and see what that stupid woman is doing,' Digby said, lifting Sam down and taking his hand. 'Probably nothing at all, as usual.'

19

Sister Veronica stood at the living-room door. She could hear Florence talking to Magnus behind her. She turned to look.

'Upstairs to bed this instant,' Florence was saying, her voice harsh and stressed. 'And don't come down until that awful stuff has worn off. And then, Magnus, we will be having some serious words. Maybe we should find a counsellor for you, I'm just not sure what the best thing to do is at the moment. No wonder your daughter is so uncontrollable, she needs you to parent her not to act like a teenager yourself. She desperately needs to be looked after by you, for boundaries to be put in place, encouragement shown, then sanctions when she steps out of line, can't you see that? Go on, off you go.'

On the way back from the greenhouse, with Magnus trailing after them like a moody teenager, Florence had explained that cannabis had always been his go-to crutch when he felt stressed. It had started at the age of fifteen, apparently, when he'd got in with a crowd of local boys during the school holidays. He'd been a shy child before that, and had relished the opportunity of making friends and 'fitting in'. After experiencing the relaxation smoking pot could bring, Magnus had been hooked, and as far as she knew, had had bouts of smoking the stuff ever since.

Turning towards the living room, Sister Veronica surveyed the scene in front of her. Christmas carols were playing in the background. Someone had had the same idea as her; make Christmas a bit more normal for everyone. Lucie was sitting with Coco on one of the sofas, and they were both looking at something on Coco's phone.

'You look very pretty in that one,' Lucie was saying. 'But is your dad happy with the outfits you wear in these Instagram photos? They're a bit skimpy.'

'He doesn't care,' Coco replied, which Sister Veronica thought was unfortunately probably true. She'd barely seen Magnus interact at all with his children since her arrival at the house. Florence was the most caring towards them. It was a sad state of affairs.

Ophelia was sitting by the window, her expression tight and still. She was still plastered in make-up, Sister Veronica noticed. Perhaps she had more bruises to hide. *Something really must be done about Digby.* As usual, there was no sign of Digby or Sam. That whole set-up really did seem so strange and unsettling.

Neil, Ryan and Nathan were squashed together on another sofa, all staring intently at their phones, not saying a word to each other. Barnaby was asleep in an armchair, and Cecily was staring at Neil and her grandsons with an expression on her face that was anything but loving. Maud was sitting on a foot stool, knitting away, and Wilfred was hanging his savage-looking Christmas decorations on the tree.

Lucie looked up and smiled at her.

'Come and sit down, Sister. Things in here are relatively calm for once,' she said, patting the chaise longue that stood next to her. 'Rufus has just left in a taxi to go and pick up Araminta. Apparently they've pumped her stomach and she's ready to come home.' She pulled a face. 'God, I hope she stays off the booze, at least for a couple of days. I'm actually really worried she'll do herself some serious harm if she doesn't.'

Sister Veronica settled herself next to Lucie and Coco. *Ah, the sound of carols*, she thought. *Almost makes me feel normal again.* She looked around at the Christmas tree, and at the holly over the fireplace, then at the tasteful decorations hung from the ceiling. *We've all forgotten how to create a festive atmosphere*, she reflected, a feeling of nostalgia pervading her, childhood memories of candles, wreaths, presents, delicious smells and pine needles coming back to her. *But then it's to be expected, under the circumstances. How can a celebration and a tragedy co-exist at the same time?*

'Is there any more news about Uncle Giles?' Lucie leaned towards her. 'I was wondering if they've found out what killed him. It's all so sad, such a shock for poor Auntie Florence. I was thinking that maybe it was a heart attack? He's always eaten and drunk far too much.'

'Er...' Sister Veronica looked at her, thinking fast. 'No, no news yet, Lucie. It may be a few days until we hear anything more.'

A noise made her look round. It was Mrs Hardman coming in, carrying a tray of steaming mugs. Behind her walked Digby and Sam. Neither looked very happy.

'Sam!' Ophelia jumped up and walked over to him, bending down to give him a big kiss.

'Hello, you stupid woman,' Sam said. His voice was almost robotic, unnatural. There was a perceptible slowing down in the room, as though everyone else's ears were opening to listen to whatever was coming next.

'What?' Ophelia stepped back. 'Don't say that to Mummy, Sam, it's very rude.'

'It's what Daddy calls you, you stupid woman,' Sam said.

A smirk rode across Digby's face.

'And he says you're selfish, and that you don't love me,' Sam said, looking up at his mother.

Lucie rose to her feet.

'I'm sorry, Ophelia. I was hoping to talk to you in private, but this really is too much,' she said, her eyes flashing angrily. 'Digby, you must be saying these things to Sam? He's too young to think of them himself.'

'Ophelia doesn't mind, do you, darling?' Digby looked at his wife. *He holds himself in such tight control*, Sister Veronica thought. *Every muscle in his body looks tense. But he's keeping his cool, he thinks it's perfectly acceptable to treat his wife in this way, and that he can just brush away anyone's concern for her. He's so righteous and arrogant.* 'She knows what Sam's talking about. Don't worry, Lucie. It's nothing that concerns you, just forget about it.'

Lucie looked at Ophelia. Her eyes were wet with tears but she was blinking fast, as though trying to look normal.

'I'm afraid it *is* my business, Digby, when I see my cousin being so horribly treated,' Lucie said, turning back to him. 'It's not the first time I've heard Sam say this type of thing to his mother. And like I said, he's too young to come up with such specific, nasty phrases on his own. They come from you, don't they?'

'I don't say anything that isn't justified, Lucie.' Digby's eyes were dark now. A muscle had begun twitching rapidly next to his right eye. *Probably not used to anyone standing up to him*, Sister Veronica thought. Her feeling of foreboding grew significantly and she dug her nails into her hands, trying to steady her emotions. 'If you're really interested, why don't you ask Ophelia about it?'

Lucie turned to her cousin who now had rivers of tears flowing down her face despite her best efforts. Some of the thick foundation she'd plastered on was coming away, exposing the remnants of the purple bruise around her eye.

'Jesus.' Lucie stepped forward, noticing at once. 'Has he hit you, Ophelia?' She leant forward to inspect the damage. Cecily, Sister Veronica noticed, was squinting at Ophelia from where she was sitting, trying to get a better view. Neil had looked up from his phone, and was looking from his wife, to Ophelia, to Digby, concern on his face. Florence, who had just entered the room, was watching the scene unfold in front of her, her mouth open. Maud had placed her knitting down on her lap, her brow now deeply furrowed.

'It's fine, really.' Ophelia was shaking. 'Please can we just leave it? I'm feeling really tired, I'm sure Sam might need a nap too. I might just...'

'No,' Lucie said firmly. 'I know you're scared but he's not going to stop unless you take back some control, Ophelia. Believe me, I've been through all this with my best friend Melody, and now I'm doing research into domestic violence. Don't enable Digby to carry on doing this to you by not taking action. You are among family now, and we'll support you. Come on, have courage.'

'It's not the first time he's hit her,' Wilfred called from the Christmas tree. 'I saw him bashing her with the bucket in the outhouse. I hate you, Digby. You're a big bully.'

Lucie looked at Ophelia.

'Is that true?' she said.

Ophelia didn't move. She seemed frozen with fear, Sister Veronica thought, her heart going out to the poor girl in front of her. She'd been planning on intervening herself – in private, of course – away from prying eyes. But sometimes situations had a habit of moving themselves on, in her experience, when no one was expecting it.

'You don't understand,' Ophelia whispered through her tears. 'It's fine, really. Can we just leave it now, please?'

'No.' Lucie's voice was getting louder. 'This man is abusing you. You bastard,' she said, turning to Digby. 'What the fuck? How dare you lay your hands on my cousin? How dare you belittle her, and teach her son to do the same? It's disgusting, and it's against the law. And it stops right now.'

Digby stared at Lucie. Something inside him seemed to visibly snap, as though her harsh words had cut through his usual control. He seemed to want to reply to her, opening and shutting his mouth, as though an internal battle was raging inside him. His face had gone very white, except for two magenta blemishes that were growing on his cheeks.

'Stop pretending you care about Ophelia,' Digby said eventually, his words coming out very fast, looking at Lucie. *Ah, we begin to see the real man behind the mask.* Sister Veronica's stomach flipped. *Lucie's broken through his self-control.* 'You're as messed up as the rest of everyone here. You're a family of lunatics, you only have to spend five minutes with the lot of you to know that. And you have no idea what Ophelia has done to make me angry, so keep your nose out of my business.'

Sister Veronica saw Ryan and Nathan eying what was going on in front of them with alarm. Neil had noticed their reaction too.

'It's all right, boys,' he said in a low voice. 'Mum's just trying to help Ophelia. It's all going to be okay.'

'Yes, we may be messed up here, Digby, but at least we don't viciously harm each other,' Lucie spat. *Other than the murderer, whoever that is,* Sister Veronica thought, looking at Digby, and wondering if it could be him. 'And I love Ophelia, she's my cousin, and I'm going to protect her from *you*.'

'Really?' Digby said, his eyebrows lowering, the magenta flush spreading throughout his face. 'You're going to protect the bitch who tricked me into having a child? Lied to me, told me she was on the pill, but had actually stopped taking it? I trusted her.' He turned to his wife, his eyes full of hatred. 'But she deceived me. She knew I didn't want a child at that stage, I was worried about money, there were redundancies going on in my department and I thought I might be next. But oh no, she didn't care about that. She misled me, treated me like a fool. She deserves to suffer for that.'

'I see,' Lucie said, looking at Ophelia, who now looked close to collapse. Sister Veronica stepped forward and guided the girl towards a chair. 'So that's what this is all about.'

'I'm so sorry, Digby,' Ophelia whispered, her shoulders drooping forwards as she sat down. 'I'm so sorry. I'll keep saying that forever if you want me to.'

'Maybe Ophelia didn't go about having a child the right way,' Lucie said, stroking her cousin's hair. 'It sounds like she should have been honest with you, gone about things more honourably. But you love Sam now, don't you, Digby?'

Digby nodded.

'Then why don't you just give yourself over to that feeling of love for him, and stop punishing your wife? I think she's suffered enough now for her mistake, don't you? You could be a happy family together. None of us are perfect, are we? Neil and I have to forgive each other for little things on a weekly basis.' Lucie glanced at her husband.

'But this isn't a *little thing*, is it?' A muscle was trembling in Digby's jaw. *He's getting very angry*, Sister Veronica thought. *I hope he doesn't do anything stupid.* 'She made a fool out of me, she used me. I can't just let go of that, she deserves to suffer every day for taking away my right, my control, about whether I have children or not.' *It's interesting how Sam isn't reacting to Digby talking about his mother in such a negative way*, Sister Veronica thought. *Probably used to it, poor little lamb. He seems so depressed. No four-year-old should look so unhappy.*

Lucie turned to Ophelia, bending over a little.

'Do you want to stay with this man, given the awful way he treats you?' she said. Ophelia's shoulders dropped down even further. They were trembling, as were her thin hands that were winding around each other in her lap, Sister Veronica noticed. 'Because if you don't we can help you and Sam move away from him.'

'Oh no, Sam will be staying with me,' Digby said loudly before Ophelia had a chance to respond. 'If Ophelia leaves me, she gives up her right to mother the boy.'

'I don't think a court will see it that way,' Lucie said, standing up again and shaking her head. 'You really are a nasty piece of work, aren't you, Digby? And by the way, you're punching way above your station with Ophelia. God knows what she ever saw in you. You seem to think you have some sort of hold over her, by using Sam against her. But the police will see right through that and place the child with her.'

'No police,' Ophelia whispered. 'Please stop now, Lucie.' She'd started rocking back and forth, very gently.

'Come on, son, these people here are as bad as your mother,' Digby said, taking hold of the white-faced boy's hand, an ounce of his former self-control appearing to return. *He obviously can't stand showing emotion in front of other people*, Sister Veronica thought, watching him carefully. *He looks embarrassed now. Angry, but embarrassed. One emotion feeds off the other.* 'Bunch of overdramatic, illogical idiots,' Digby muttered. Within seconds he'd led Sam from the room, and the scene was over as quickly as it had started.

'Where's he taking Sam?' Ophelia looked up, her voice rising in panic. 'Don't let him take Sam away.'

Lucie went over to the door and stuck her head out.

'They're just going upstairs,' she said, a soothing quality in her voice. 'Don't worry, Digby's not taking Sam out of the house. It gets dark so early now. He's probably gone to lick his wounds in private.'

'You don't understand.' Ophelia's eyes were wild. 'He's always threatened to take my son away from me. He'll be so angry you stood up to him in front of everyone, he's bound to do that now. Why did you do that, Lucie? Why did you ruin everything? Do you know how hard I've worked to stay with Sam? How much abuse I've had to put up with? Now it's all been for nothing.'

20

Cecily watched as the old busybody nun, Florence and her daughter Lucie led the hysterical Ophelia from the room.

'Let's go somewhere more private to talk,' Florence was saying, her arm round her niece's waist. 'Digby's not taking Sam anywhere at the moment, they're both safely upstairs. You don't have to worry. Come on. Try to relax a bit.'

'You don't understand, Aunt Florence,' Ophelia said, her voice coming out in gasps. 'You don't know what he's capable of.'

She saw Neil jump up, walk over and lay his hand on Lucie's arm as she went through the doorway after her cousin and aunt, trying to get his wife's attention.

'I'm taking the boys home now,' he said, as Lucie turned towards him. His face had an anger in it. 'That scene was the last straw. The boys are really upset, Luce. It's nearly Christmas Eve, and instead of relaxing and getting excited, today they've seen their aunt Araminta lying in a drunken unconscious mess at the bottom of the stairs, and now you having an argument with an abusive man. It's too much. They shouldn't have to see all this, it's not what Christmas is about.'

'No,' Lucie whispered. 'No, Neil, please. I haven't had a chance to talk to Auntie Florence yet.'

'It doesn't matter,' Neil said, stroking Lucie's shoulder. 'Come with us, Luce. Let's get out of here and create a happy Christmas for the boys at home like we normally do.'

'I can't go yet, Neil, I have to talk to Auntie Florence about the money or we will just be in a deeper mess.' Lucie's voice was breaking. 'Just give me a bit longer.'

'No,' Neil said, his voice firm. 'Don't worry about the money. Just contact the university and ask to put your PhD on hold for a few months. Then you can get a job, we can pay off the bills and debts, and then you can start your studies up again.'

'I can't.' Lucie was shaking her head. 'I've already asked my uni, Neil, and they said I can't take another break, that they've already extended the end date of my research to the maximum time.'

'Then put your family first for once and stop doing the PhD.' A fierceness entered Neil's voice. He took his hand away from her shoulder. 'Instead of trying to do good for everyone else, do what's right for us.'

A tear ran down Lucie's cheek.

'I thought you understood, Neil? I thought you said you'd support me?' she said, her voice thick with emotion.

'I *do* understand and I *did* say that,' he said. 'But I never knew that you stopping work would lead us to such financial ruin. I'm doing all the overtime I can, Luce, I can't do any more. It's killing me as it is. But it's not enough. Our credit history is already ruined with us not being able to make payments. We'll end up with county court judgements, and bailiffs coming to our door. Is that what you want?'

'No,' Lucie said, sniffing. She exhaled. 'Fine. Take the boys home and I'll try and talk to Auntie Florence this evening, then I'll follow you back, I'll get a late-night train or ask someone to give me a lift or something. At the very latest I'll be back tomorrow morning. I just need to give it one more shot, see if she'll lend us some money. If she can't, I'll talk to my supervisors about stopping my studies.'

Neil leant forward and kissed her.

'Okay,' he said. 'I'll ring you when we get back. It shouldn't take us too long.'

Oh for God's sake, not another drama, Cecily thought, watching Lucie leave the room, her head bowed. *Well that's what you get, Lucinda, for marrying a common as muck warehouse worker. No money. If you'd married someone from a* proper *family like Araminta did, then he'd have been able to pay for as many PhDs as you liked. That's just the way of the world. But you were always a little socialist, weren't you?*

She turned her attention to Wilfred, who was hanging his last dinosaur on the tree.

'Do you like them?' he asked, noticing her interest.

'No,' Cecily said with conviction. 'I think they're revolting.'

'Thank you.' Wilfred smiled. 'They're meant to be. After all, they're vicious prehistoric beasts.'

Cecily rolled her eyes and turned towards her husband. His eyes had briefly opened during the Digby and Lucie spat, but had since closed again. He was omitting a gentle snore. *Honestly, life must be so simple for that man*, she thought. *All he does is exist, with everyone else running around making things easy for him.* The tediousness of Barnaby jolted a sudden pang of grief for Giles deep inside her. *It had never been boring with him*, she thought, *he'd been a live wire, always the life and soul of any room.* Cecily wasn't usually given to having strong feelings about anyone, but the tug of longing she now experienced for her former lover took her by surprise. She'd love to see him walk into the room just one more time. Liven everyone up with some controversial remarks, shake things up a bit.

She looked around, hoping for a distraction away from her ruminations. The three teenagers, Ryan, Nathan and Coco, were all sitting around gaping at their phones, their faces still and gormless. She saw Maud put her knitting down and get up and follow Mrs Hardman out of the room. *Well, if there's nothing exciting going on I'm going to fix myself a drink*, Cecily thought, rising elegantly to her feet. *No point sitting around missing Giles and wishing things were different.* She'd been to finishing school, demanded to go, in fact, until her hard-working middle-class parents had caved in, and always remembered what she'd been taught about the right way for a lady to sit down and stand up. *Appearances and the impression you give are so important*, she mused. *Not that anyone here seems to realise that.*

Intent on going down to the wine cellar and seeing what goodies she could find, she stepped out into the hall. A white envelope was lying on the mat by the front door.

That's strange, she thought. *The postman has already been today – I saw Florence scoop up a couple of Christmas cards from the floor earlier.* She walked over and picked it up. There was just one word written in nondescript capitals across the front: FLORENCE.

21

Mrs Hardman banged the saucepan on to the stove a little harder than she would normally. *This household, honestly. They are the talk of the village, with all their strange ways.* She only stayed working for them because of kind Mrs Beresford, Florence, who had always looked after her and paid her generously even when she'd had time off to look after her sick mother two years ago. But seeing dramatic scenes like the one that had just unfolded in the living room between that awful Digby and Lucie was commonplace, in her experience. Why couldn't the family just learn to get along?

She opened the fridge and retrieved a variety of colourful vegetables from one of the shelves, thinking of her own dear husband, Patrick. Oh, they'd had their ups and downs over the years but nothing like the stuff that went on at Chalfield Hall. She thought of her two children, Claire and Freddie – both of them had flown the nest now, bless them – and how lucky she was to have such good, kind children, who always checked up on her and sent her money whenever they had any spare. Nothing like that pathetic Magnus, who never seemed to be able to get his life in order. Or that revolting Araminta, who was never shy of showing how superior she felt to Mrs Hardman. Lucie was all right, although she could be a bit stressy at times. Poor Ophelia, well. She was one Mrs Hardman *did* feel sorry for. It wasn't her place to intrude and ask too many questions, but she hoped the family would do something to help the girl, now they knew the truth about her awful marriage. Cecily was so obnoxious she could hardly look at the woman and Barnaby didn't seem like his head was ever on this planet. The old nun seemed okay, although Mrs Hardman had caught her staring at her a few times, with Sister Veronica's eyes seemingly boring in to her soul. Maybe she didn't get out of her convent much and had forgotten it was rude to stare at people, she reflected.

Slicing the vegetables up quickly with the expertise of an experienced cook, Mrs Hardman's mind returned to the matter that had been troubling her since Mr Beresford – Giles – had collapsed and died. Being a very discreet and private person herself, she was not in the habit of snooping into other people's business. It was part of what made her such a good house-keeper. However, before everyone had arrived at Chalfield Hall for Christmas, she had unwittingly witnessed a disturbing sight. Being the official cleaner of the ground floor – with Mrs Beresford in charge of upstairs hygiene – she'd arrived at the study door one day, duster and spray in her hands, believing – because of the quietness in the house – that Mr and Mrs Beresford were out. So she'd been very startled to find Giles Beresford hunched over his desk with his back to her, his hands tightly clenching big tufts of his hair either side of his head. He'd been staring at his computer screen, which – from the brief glance she'd got – looked like some sort of online banking page. Unaware of her presence behind him, he'd suddenly started making the strangest noise: a cross between a primitive animalistic howl and an agony-filled groan. Then, still holding clumps of his hair, he'd begun to shake his head from side to side. He'd been the picture of a man in some sort of mental anguish.

Shocked at the sight before her, Mrs Hardman had tiptoed back to the kitchen as quietly as she could. She'd never had much time for the pompous Mr Beresford, and fully intended to forget about the strange situation very quickly, deciding to go back and clean the study at a later point. Whatever was troubling the man was his own business, she'd thought at the time. No need for her to think anything more about it.

That was until Mr Beresford had collapsed and died. Ever since hearing the news, Mrs Hardman had been in two minds about telling Mrs Beresford what she'd witnessed that day. The understated professional side of her felt she should keep her nose out of everyone's business, and keep her mouth shut. But the compassionate side of her, that ached for Mrs Beresford whenever she saw her upset and grieving, suggested that it might be an idea to share the information with her. It was probably nothing, but it might help somehow. What if Mr Beresford had been so upset about whatever it was on his screen that he'd become so stressed he'd had a heart attack? At least if she shared her information it might give Mrs Beresford a tiny jigsaw piece of the puzzle regarding her husband's state of mind, leading up to his death. *No*, she thought for the umpteenth time, *best to keep out of it all. Let them get on with it themselves.* Although, she vacillated quickly back again, would she always feel guilty if she said nothing?

She went over to the fridge again and retrieved a large hunk of beef, slapping it down on to the chopping board. *I'll keep thinking as I cook*, she decided. *Then the right thing to do might well come to me.*

22

Sister Veronica leaned over as Florence ripped open the envelope. Cecily had thrust it at her cousin before disappearing through the door that led to the wine cellar. She'd reappeared a few minutes later holding two bottles of wine and exited the kitchen towards the hall looking very pleased with herself. They'd settled Ophelia down with a hot chocolate before Cecily's arrival, and had listened with grave concern to what she'd told them about Digby.

'Don't you worry, my dear,' Florence had said after she'd finished talking, giving her niece a hug. 'We won't let Digby take Sam away from this house, and we won't let the two of you go back with him. You can stay with me as long as you need to – goodness knows this place is big enough. In a minute, I'll lock the front and back doors and carry the keys with me in my pockets. That way, no one will be able to leave the house without my knowledge, okay?'

Ophelia had nodded, with a look of doubt on her now blotchy face. Her breathing had slowed and some colour was slowly returning to her cheeks.

'I'm so sorry you've had to go through this on your own,

Ophelia,' Sister Veronica had said, reaching out to pat the girl's hand. 'What an ordeal. It's over now, we all know what Digby's been up to. If you want to press charges against him we can call the police here. But there's no rush to do that,' she said quickly, seeing tears well up in Ophelia's eyes again. 'Just relax now, and drink your hot chocolate.'

Leaving the girl to have a minute or two of peace and quiet in the kitchen by herself, she and Florence had traipsed up to Florence's bedroom to open the letter in private, making sure all the doors were locked and the keys removed and safely placed in Florence's skirt pocket on the way.

'It's another one of those awful letters,' Florence said, sighing, as she drew out the white paper and opened it up. 'Looks like whoever is behind them isn't going to stop just because Giles is dead.'

'Yes, I thought it was going to be one of those awful things as soon as I saw the envelope.' Sister Veronica leaned forward. '"It's up to you to put things right, Florence. Do it now, before anyone else has to die",' she read.

'It's a threat.' Florence's hands began to shake. 'It must be from whoever killed Giles. Oh, V, I can't stand this anymore. I need to get away from this house.' She walked across the room, wringing her hands in front of her. 'I've had enough of being stoic, I can't do it now.'

Sister Veronica sat down heavily on the beautifully embroidered bedspread.

'I know how you feel, Flo,' she said. 'I'm scared, too, mostly for you. This is a very nasty business indeed. But I'm not sure leaving Chalfield Hall right now would be the wisest move to make.'

'Why not?' Florence spun round, her eyes wild. 'Surely it would be the most sensible thing to do? Giles has gone, V, most probably murdered by someone who is in my house right now.

Why should I become a sitting duck, waiting for whoever it is to strike again? I'm exhausted, V. I just want some peace, so I can grieve for my husband without having this stress to worry about. Is that too much to ask?'

'No, of course it's not,' Sister Veronica said. She was making an effort to keep her voice calm and soothing for her cousin's sake, but inside her a sense of terror was rising. Someone had continued to threaten Florence so soon after her husband died, and it was a sick and cowardly thing to do. The fact that most of the people at Chalfield were unaware that Giles had been killed as opposed to dying from natural causes meant that they were slightly safer, that the murderer thought he or she was still operating incognito from most people for now. But the assassin would also suspect that the hospital would probably have identified the cause of death through the toxicology testing, and would have told Florence the results. The detective and police officer turning up earlier would have confirmed this. And the fact that Florence had noticeably shared private words with Sister Veronica on several occasions put them both in great danger. The killer would know she and Florence were aware of them, even if their true identity was not yet known. But escaping from the house now would only prolong the situation. What they needed to do was bring it to a head, find out who was sending the letters and who murdered Giles, and end the horrible business once and for all.

'I wish I hadn't invited everyone here,' Florence said, her face full of agony. 'If I hadn't, Giles might well still be alive. He and I could be enjoying Christmas like we usually do, instead of having this bloody nightmare to deal with. This is all my fault.'

'No, Flo, of course it's not your fault.' Sister Veronica stood up and went to embrace her cousin in a tight hug. 'All right, so if someone secretly wanted to commit a murder, then a closed family gathering provides the perfect place. But how on earth were you meant to know that someone was heinous enough to be planning such a thing? It's not your fault at all, and you mustn't start blaming yourself.'

A floorboard creaked outside Florence's bedroom door. Their heads snapped round at the same time. Soft footsteps padded away and a door closed quietly further down the passage.

Sister Veronica strode over and flung the door open at once. She peered up and down the dark corridor. Had someone been listening to their conversation? The murderer? Now whoever it was would know everything they'd been discussing. The dashed feeling of foreboding in her reached new critical levels and a cold sweat broke out across her forehead.

'You go downstairs, Flo, to see who's there,' she said, thinking fast. 'I'll go and look in each bedroom to see who's up here. But be careful. Call out if anything happens.'

With a pounding heart she stepped out onto the landing, watching her cousin make her way down the sweeping staircase, knowing that within minutes she may discover the identity of Giles' killer, who was possibly the sender of the poisonous letters too.

23

It was a very long corridor, that travelled the entire width of the large house, with most of the bedrooms spanning off it on either side. Underneath, spreading out along the ground floor, was the large semicircular hall, the front living room, the generous kitchen, the dining room, the old creepy back living room that mad old Henrietta used to hold court in – unused by anyone nowadays – the study, pantry and various store rooms and cupboards. The lights were brighter downstairs, on the whole. But up in the corridor, the lights on the walls provided only a dim sepulchral glow.

Sister Veronica, her heart beating fast, stopped at the first door and listened. Loud, thumping music was coming from within. She looked down and saw that there was a sign sporting the words 'Private: Do Not Enter' hanging from the door handle. She knocked, nevertheless, and went in. Coco was lying on her bed, staring at a sheet of paper in front of her, a pencil in her hand. Beautifully intricate drawings covered her wall, depicting magical forests, landscapes and different types of animals. They were stunning compositions showing real talent. The girl looked up.

'Oh my *God*,' Coco said loudly, her voice back to its petulant whine. 'Can't you read? It says *do not enter* on my door. Are you blind or something? I've just come up here to be by myself and get away from you losers. *Go away*.' She turned her head back to her paper again, and Sister Veronica gladly shut the door.

She approached the next room, this time on the other side of the corridor, and listened. Someone was moving around inside. She knocked, and opened the door.

'Oh hello, Sister,' Neil said. He looked flustered. A rucksack was on the bed and a messy pile of clothes lay next to it. 'I'm going to take Ryan and Nathan home now, back to Milton Keynes. Luce and I thought it best, what with everything that's going on here. They're not having fun, and it doesn't make any sense to ruin their Christmas any more than need be.'

'I quite understand,' Sister Veronica said, shooting him a quick smile. 'Sorry for the intrusion, I'm just looking for Florence.'

'I saw her downstairs a while ago,' Neil called, as she closed the door.

She knew who the next room belonged to even before she opened the door. The potent herby smell became even stronger after she knocked and went in.

'Sorry, Magnus,' she said to the prone figure on the bed. 'I'm looking for your mother.' He didn't reply, just lay very still staring at the window. He wasn't smoking anything, Sister Veronica saw, which was a relief. *Poor Florence, the things her cousin has to put up with. The smell must be a residual one from his clothes.* She closed the door and walked on.

A huge waft of lily-of-the-valley perfume assaulted her nose as she reached the next door. It was a very welcome antidote to Magnus' lingering cannabis stench. She knocked, and entered.

'Ah, hello, Maud,' Sister Veronica said, looking at the rosy-cheeked lady sitting in a chair by the window, a pile of pink knitting on her knee. 'Sorry to disturb you, I'm looking for Florence. Have you seen her?'

'No, dear,' Maud said, looking up. 'Not since that fuss downstairs with Digby. What a carry on that was.'

Sister Veronica closed the door and walked on. Everyone was up here, it seemed, which didn't really help narrow down who'd been listening at Florence's door.

The next door was open. The room inside was empty and chaotic. The bedsheets were pulled halfway off the bed, clothes were scattered all over the floor, and empty glasses and wine bottles littered all available surfaces. *Ah*, she thought. *Looks like Rufus and Araminta's room. They should be back from the hospital any minute now.*

She walked on, and knocked at the next door, then turned the handle. She saw Sam first, sitting on the edge of his small camp bed, his face white and serious. He looked at her. Digby was packing symmetrically folded clothes into an open suitcase laid out on the double bed.

'Can I help you?' He turned towards her, his tone cold and unfriendly.

'Er, no, sorry, just looking for Florence.' Sister Veronica backed away, closing the door. *Aha, so the man* is *planning to make an escape with Sam.* She'd have to flag that up with Florence and Ophelia in just a second, after she'd checked the last three rooms. It wouldn't take her long to do. Walking past her own bedroom, she stopped and knocked at the next door, before opening it.

'Do you mind?' Cecily looked up. She was sitting on one of the two twin beds inside, a glass of something red in her hand. 'It's rude to barge into other people's rooms, you know, Sister.'

'Terribly sorry, Cecily,' Sister Veronica said, backing out. 'Just looking for Florence.'

'Well she's hardly going to be in *my* bedroom is she?' she heard Cecily call, a sneering quality in her voice.

A sound behind her made her turn. Ophelia had just arrived at the top of the stairs, and was making for her room. She looked like a ghost, pale and ethereal.

'Are you sure you want to go in there, my dear?' Sister Veronica called in a low voice. 'After everything that just happened?'

'I need to make sure Sam's okay,' Ophelia said, turning the handle to her room. She went in, closing the door quietly behind her. Sister Veronica sent out a quick prayer for Ophelia's safety to the universe, before turning back to the last two doors. She knocked on one and opened it. There was no one there. Muddy clothes covered the twin beds in front of her and a rugby ball was balanced on the dresser. *Ah*, she thought, closing the door again. *Ryan and Nathan's room. They must be downstairs, or out in the garden.*

Just the last door to go. She knocked and opened it.

'Hello,' Wilfred said, sounding cheery. He was sitting at his desk, a large computer screen in front of him. 'I'm just playing digital solitaire. Is dinner ready yet?'

'Er, no, I think it's still a bit too early for that.' Sister Veronica smiled in spite of her fear. 'Sorry to bother you, Wilfred, I'm just looking for your aunt, Florence.'

'No idea where she is, sorry.' Wilfred turned back to his screen as she shut the door tightly.

Well, that's no help, Sister Veronica thought, trundling back down the corridor towards the staircase. *Nearly everyone's in their rooms.*

Minutes later, she walked into the kitchen.

'V, did you find anything?' Florence said, turning round. Behind her was a large window, and through it lay the darkening garden. 'I didn't find many people down here, just Lucie, Ryan and Nathan. Oh yes, and Barnaby, who's asleep in the living room as usual. Mrs Hardman has just gone to the outhouse to get something. Ophelia was here, but I think she went upstairs.'

'Yes, I saw her going into her room.' Sister Veronica frowned. 'Digby and Sam are in there. I hope she's going to be all right. That man really is a disgusting excuse for a human being. The sooner we get him out of the house, the better. He's packing his suitcase, Flo. I saw a teddy bear in there so it looks like he's intending to take Sam away after all. I didn't say anything at the time in case it made him angry again. Ophelia was right. We need to do something, we can't let him take the boy away, he's not fit to look after any child.'

Sister Veronica would never forget the horror of what happened next. The yell, the sickening thump that sounded like it came from the entrance hall. Then a second crash. The sight of Digby that she and Florence encountered, after they'd hurried towards the noise, splatted like an insect on the hall carpet. He was lying on his back, Sister Veronica saw, as she walked towards him, his eyes open but very still, blood oozing from them, as well as from his nose, mouth and ears. His neck was twisted sideways. There was a look of shock on his face. One of his legs was bent backwards at an unnatural angle. Sister Veronica looked up quickly. Right above him, at the top of the sweeping staircase, was the exposed part of the landing that led to the corridor with all the bedrooms. A low rail was the only safety device along it, a cursory effort to stop people from falling. If she had to guess, it looked like Digby had fallen – or been pushed – over the rail. The suitcase he'd been packing lay wide open near his feet, its contents splayed out messily over the hall floor. That had caused the second crash, she reckoned. Someone throwing that over after him. She recognised the teddy bear she'd seen inside it, now lying next to the Christmas tree. She knelt down and tried to feel for a pulse in his wrist, then his neck.

'Flo,' she said, looking up at her cousin. 'I think Digby's dead.'

24

'I'm phoning for an ambulance.' Florence's hand shook as she retrieved her mobile phone from her pocket. 'And I'm going to ask the police to come too.'

She dialled three nines and turned away to speak as the call handler answered. Most of the family were emerging after hearing the noise, Sister Veronica noticed as she looked around, with Wilfred, Neil, Maud, and Cecily – still holding her wine glass – taking up shocked stances on the stairs. Ophelia had appeared at the top by the very rail her husband had just tumbled over to his death. Her face was still, unreadable, her eyes trained downwards on the body that used to belong to Digby. Her arm was stretched out, as though preventing someone from coming further along the corridor. *Sam*, Sister Veronica thought. *Yes, don't let the poor boy see his father like this.*

Ryan and Nathan emerged from the living room, phones in their hands. They stopped when they saw what was going on, shock freezing their expressions.

'What's happened?' Ryan mumbled.

'Right, boys, let's go outside.' Neil pushed past Cecily, Maud and Wilfred and jogged down the stairs. 'It's time we got in the car and made our way home. I don't want you spending any more time in this house of horrors. Mum can bring the rest of your stuff with her when she comes back. You've got your phones, I see, that's all you need to bring really, isn't it? Come on, let's go.'

He paused next to Lucie, who had walked up the corridor from the dining room, giving her a brief kiss on the lips. For a moment, they stared into each other's eyes.

'Come home soon, Luce,' he said. 'We need you there. But the boys have seen enough now. We're going.' *Lucie and Neil are much more protective of their boys than anyone is over Wilfred and Coco*, Sister Veronica mused. *Wilfred gets to see everything that goes on in this house, totally uncensored. No wonder he's so dissociated from his emotions, I think I would be if I lived here full time. It's a survival strategy – holding everything at arm's length so it doesn't touch or hurt you.*

Lucie nodded, unable to talk, walking over to squeeze her sons goodbye. Florence retrieved the key from her pocket and threw it to Neil, who opened the front door. Rufus and Araminta were standing on the doorstep.

'Hello, old chap,' Rufus said, giving Neil a broad grin. 'The prodigal drinker returns.' He jabbed his thumb towards his wife. 'Right, let's get the mince pies out and have a sherry, shall we?' He paused, looking around. 'What's everyone looking so miserable about?' His eyes took in the scene behind Neil. His mouth opened slightly. 'What the bloody hell's been going on here?'

'Goodbye, Rufus.' Neil walked smartly past him. 'Come on, lads, let's get going.' Muttering muted goodbyes, Ryan and Nathan followed their father out. In seconds, they'd disappeared round the side of the house, heading for the large gravelled area where all the cars were parked.

'Christ.' Araminta went a shade of yellow as she peered through the front door. She made a heaving motion as though she was about to vomit. 'What happened to Digby? I don't think I can handle this. I've been throwing up all day as it is.'

'It looks like he fell over the upstairs railings,' Sister Veronica said, standing up from her kneeling position and turning towards her. 'Either he jumped, which in my opinion is very unlikely given that he'd just packed his suitcase and was planning to take Sam back home, or he was pushed. He's dead. Your aunt has just phoned the emergency services. No one must touch his body, or move anything. This is a crime scene now.' *And the only person with a strong motive is Ophelia*, she thought. *The girl just walked into her bedroom to find her abusive husband about to take her son away from her, and minutes later the man is found dead? Seems like too much of a coincidence to me. Although Ophelia is such a slight little thing. Would she have the strength to heave him over the railings? Well, people can find resources in them they never knew they had when they're feeling passionate enough about something.* She tried not to look up at Ophelia, she didn't want to draw any attention to the girl. Florence, having now finished on the phone, seemed to be also trying not to look up at her niece, but her head kept twitching upwards. *Even if she did do it*, Sister Veronica reflected, *surely it would be classed as self-defence or manslaughter and she wouldn't get in too much trouble? I mean, there are enough of us who witnessed the man's abuse towards her.*

'Doesn't look like there are many of us left now,' Rufus said, his face now grave, as he ushered his wife in and closed the front door. 'We started out as a party of eighteen, if my calculations are correct. Twenty if you include Mrs Hardman and sad old Romilly. What with poor Giles and Digby, and Neil and the boys leaving, we're down to fifteen. Thirteen really, as on reflection Romilly doesn't count, she doesn't live here, thank God, and I can't responsibly include Mrs Hardman in the headcount even if she is a fantastic cook.'

Magnus appeared at the top of the stairs, his hair a mess, his paunch sticking out from under his T-shirt.

'What's going on?' he said, rubbing his eyes.

'Digby's dead,' Florence said. 'Go and have a coffee, and for God's sake, Magnus, don't smoke any more of those disgusting drugs. The police will be here soon and we'll need everyone as compos mentis as possible. They'll want to interview all of us, I think. Where's Coco by the way? I haven't seen her for a while.'

'She's in her room listening to music,' Sister Veronica said. 'At least she was just before I came down to the kitchen. Maybe it's so loud she didn't hear the commotion.'

'Let's leave her up there for as long as possible,' Florence said, turning. 'The last thing we need is Coco becoming histrionic and making this already horrific situation even worse.'

Sister Veronica nodded. She looked around.

'This really is a tragic state of affairs,' she said. 'If he intended to commit suicide, why would he also throw his suitcase down? That just doesn't make sense.' She allowed her eyes to flash up to Ophelia's. The girl was still frozen, staring down at her husband's body, as though in a trance. She wasn't showing any perceptible reaction to Sister Veronica's words. What if it hadn't been her who'd pushed the man? What if it had been someone else? But that didn't add up, Ophelia was the only one who would benefit from Digby being out of the way.

'Who would have done it?' Araminta said, holding her stomach. She and her husband hadn't been there during Lucie and Digby's spat, Sister Veronica remembered. 'Rufie and I have only just arrived back. We weren't here when Digby fell, so that counts us out.'

'And I think we can safely say Sam is discounted,' Lucie said, folding her arms. 'Auntie Florence and Sister Veronica were in the kitchen talking when it happened, I heard their voices as I was downstairs, too, so were Ryan and Nathan. I'm pretty sure

Barnaby is still asleep in the living room. Mrs Hardman was going to the outhouse, I saw her walk past the window, so that just leaves the people who were upstairs. Neil, Maud, Coco, Ophelia, Cecily, Magnus and Wilfred.'

'It wasn't me,' Wilfred called from the stairs. 'I know I said I hated him, but I'd admit it if I'd done it. Didn't think of it, actually, I was too busy playing a game on my computer.'

'I think we should leave the investigating to the police,' Florence said, looking up at him. 'This really is the most hellish Christmas anyone could ever imagine.'

Ophelia said something, but it was too soft for Sister Veronica to hear.

'What did you say, dear?' she called up to her.

'I said, I've just been given the best Christmas present of my life,' Ophelia said, without taking her eyes from her husband's body. A look of relaxation was slowly working its way across her face.

25

Silence immediately spread throughout the hall, as everyone's eyes turned to focus on Ophelia. She looked up. 'I'm glad Digby is gone,' she said, as if coming to. 'But I didn't do it. I didn't kill him. I was still in the bedroom with Sam when he wheeled his suitcase out.'

'Er, like I said, dear.' Florence looked up, sounding flustered. 'Let's not say anything now that we might regret later. We're all in a state of shock, none of us know what to think or do. Let's leave it to the police to get on with the detective work, shall we, and try and keep our thoughts about the matter to ourselves?' *She's trying to protect Ophelia*, Sister Veronica thought, feeling a flash of love for her cousin. *She's trying to stop her saying anything else incriminating in front of everyone. Flo must have come to the same conclusion that I did, that Ophelia is the only person with a strong enough motive to kill Digby. But the idea of that girl heaving that weaselly man over the railing by herself is hard to imagine.*

'Well, I'm going to have another drink.' Cecily turned, making her way back up the stairs. 'This is not a Christmas anymore, it's a nightmare. And my only consolation is your stupendously wonderful wine cellar, Florence.'

'Help yourself, dear.' Florence waved a hand vaguely in the air, as Cecily disappeared along the top corridor. *Like mother, like daughter*, Sister Veronica thought. *Perhaps alcoholism runs in the family.*

'Is that a siren I hear outside?' Florence said, turning towards the front door as a familiar wailing sound permeated the air.

Minutes later, the hall was full of men and women wearing the striking uniform of the emergency services. Police officers divided the family up to take statements from them, removing each person away to a different room, and the paramedics confirmed to Sister Veronica – as she waited in the hall for her turn to give a statement – that yes, Digby was indeed dead, what with his neck being broken.

DI Ahuja arrived and took in the scene with one glance. He did not look happy.

'A second unexplained death occurring in the same house within twenty-four hours,' he said, shaking his head. 'What are the chances?'

Sister Veronica nodded, thinking that it was highly unlikely to be the same person who murdered both Giles and Digby. If her suspicions were correct, and Ophelia had somehow sent her husband falling to his death after finding out he was about to take her son away, then that was one thing. But what possible reason would she have had for killing Giles? It just didn't make sense. And could it really be her sending those awful poison pen letters to her aunt Florence? That didn't make sense either. Hadn't Flo said that the letters always arrived on the doormat when she was out shopping in the village? It sounded like someone local must be sending them, someone who could keep an eye on her movements. Digby and Ophelia didn't live anywhere near Little Ashby, as far as she was aware, and it was hardly conceivable that the girl would be driving back and forth for hours, keeping tabs on her aunt's movements. Especially not when Digby's control over her was taken into consideration. Was it really possible that there was more than one killer in the house? The very notion sent chills throughout her brain. She thought of her convent longingly. All right, so things weren't always easy there, at the Convent of the Christian Heart; she and the other sisters had been through their own personal dramas over the years, what with one thing and another. But being in this house was something else. She'd hoped – following Digby's demise – that the feeling of foreboding that had tormented her since her arrival at Chalfield would be abating. But it was still there, still pumping away with force in her mind and body. She now gave it more credit than before, almost respected it, worrying as that was for her. It seemed to be a warning signal, guiding her through the darkness, letting her know that more horror may be in store. But she didn't think she could take any more terror and suspense, her body felt quite weak all of a sudden, and memories of her cosy convent bedroom flooded her mind. *No, V*, she cautioned herself, standing up a little straighter. *Think of Flo. You must stay here, for her, or she'll have no one to look after her. Take courage, and dig down deeply for strength.* She sent a prayer out to the universe, asking for a new dose of grit, explaining to anyone that was listening that she seemed to be running low on the last one.

A noise above her, footsteps moving fast, made her look up. Coco had appeared, and was leaning over the banisters, taking in the scene below her, her long ringlets falling down; Digby's mangled body, the plethora of police officers and paramedics, the suitcase and its scattered items that still lay where they'd fallen. She opened her mouth and let out a blood-curdling scream.

Magnus appeared immediately at the living-room door.

'Coco,' he shouted up at his daughter, his voice sounding

stronger than Sister Veronica had ever heard it. 'For once in your life, SHUT THE HELL UP!'

26

Later that evening, when the police officers and paramedics had gone, and Digby's body had been taken away, most of the remaining family members sat in the living room, duvets and blankets covering their knees, nearly all of them nursing a mug of hot chocolate. Sister Veronica had overheard a muttered remark DI Ahuja had made to an officer as they left the house: 'The problem is,' he'd said, 'that no one here has a bloody alibi. No one at all. Everyone seemed to be on their own at the time. And I'll bet my hat that that man didn't jump over the rail on purpose. We need to dig deeper into this, find out how the hell that man ended up on the hall floor.'

Everyone in the living room was quiet, lost in their own thoughts, absorbing the shocking events of the last few hours. People did keep shooting looks at Ophelia, Sister Veronica noticed. It seemed the unspoken general consensus that she had somehow killed her brute of a husband, although goodness knows where she'd found the strength. There was an air of protection around her, as everyone understood the motive, but still felt traumatised by the event. After all, killing someone was such a heinous thing to do, whatever the circumstance. It was as though a force field had appeared around the girl, no one wanted to go too near her, but at the same time were treating her with renewed respect. At one point, clearly desperate to bring a touch of normality to their lives and unable to bear the silence, Lucie got up and put the carols back on, saying nothing was going to stop a ray of Christmas shining through this hellish household. 'Hark! The Herald Angels Sing' began to croon quietly away in the background.

The two youngest were the only ones not present; Sam was tucked up in bed at last, and Wilfred had announced he was going back to his room to play solitaire on his computer. Ophelia was sitting quietly, slightly away from the rest of her family, a patchwork quilt tucked neatly around her knees. The stress and strain Sister Veronica had become so accustomed to seeing on her face was leaving, a new animation taking its place. *She looks more alive than ever before*, Sister Veronica thought. *How amazing. Digby had taken the light out of her, and now that he's gone – it's coming back. It's almost magical to observe. I just can't think badly of her, if it was her who pushed him. But neither can I reconcile the fact that I've just seen Digby's dead body. The whole scenario has taken the stuffing out of me. And the fear of being here with someone who murdered Giles is fatiguing. The rest of the family don't know he was poisoned yet, just Florence and I. How long will this nightmare last?*

Coco, surpassing all previous expectations of her, had actually listened to her father when he'd bellowed at her to shut up earlier. She'd stopped screaming, a look of puzzlement taking over her face, as she absorbed the fact that her usually inert father was being assertive. She'd been rather quiet ever since. *Perhaps that's just what the girl needs*, Sister Veronica thought, glancing at her. *A firm fatherly hand. Perhaps she's been unconsciously crying out for it, what with all her grating screaming and erratic behaviour. Negative attention is better than none at all, if that's all you can get. If Magnus can keep it up, it will do their relationship no end of favours. I rather think there's hope for the girl yet.* And the drawings on her bedroom wall, that she'd only briefly glanced at when she was trying to find out who'd been outside Florence's door, were stunning. If Coco had done them herself it meant the girl had real talent. She must talk to her about them soon, show an interest and encourage her talent.

The door opened, and Maud came in with a fresh tray of hot chocolate and biscuits. Mrs Hardman had been allowed to go home after giving her statement to the police, and for once Maud had taken charge of the kettle. Florence was too drained to do anything other than rest on the sofa with her eyes closed, and Sister Veronica's body still felt weak, as though it had been pummelled from the inside. She was exhausted, she suspected, from the hyper-vigilance she'd experienced since arriving at Chalfield Hall, the growing fear, and the terror – still there – at living with a person, or people, who intended harm. And the pressure of not being able to talk about it with anyone other than Florence. She leaned forward, thanking Maud for the steaming mug, and doing a quick search for custard creams among the assorted pile on the plate.

Magnus was staring at his phone. Still pale and dishevelled-looking, his shoulders were more upright than usual and he was no longer slouching apathetically into the sofa. There was a definite air of renewed purpose surrounding him, Sister Veronica noticed with surprise.

'There's a job going in Kettering,' he said to no one in particular. 'I might apply for that. It's in sales. Looks interesting.'

The public show of his use of cannabis, and the fact that his mother and relatives now knew he was using it again as a coping mechanism, a crutch, rather than dealing with life head-on, seemed to have awoken something within him, Sister Veronica reflected. Perhaps Florence's words about him needing to parent his children properly rather than act like a teenager himself had also had an effect. And, of course, the shock of seeing Digby dead on the floor would have jolted him, showed him how quickly one can lose the opportunity of being a parent or a child, how important it was not to take any relationship for granted. The rest he'd had upstairs after Florence had extracted him from the floor of the greenhouse seemed to have been some sort of turning point. Maybe his mother's obvious disappointment and despair had played a part too. Perhaps, she thought, he'd needed something like that to happen, an intervention, for him to take a good, hard look at where his life was going. It was strange, she thought, how things like that happened. People sometimes needed a change to occur for them to turn a corner, one that gave them a metaphorical kick in the right direction.

'Sounds fantastic,' she said, managing a smile in Magnus' direction. 'I'm sure you'd do very well in the role.'

'Sounds tedious if you ask me,' Cecily said loudly. She drained the remnants of her previous hot chocolate – that she'd insisted on adding a generous amount of liqueur to – and accepted a fresh mug from Maud that quickly got the same treatment. Sister Veronica wasn't sure how many bottles of wine Cecily had worked through that evening, but she was sure it was at least two, possibly three. The woman had less inhibitions than usual, her speech was slurring, and she was dropping some of her airs and graces, at times being downright rude to anyone who took her fancy. Usually, Sister Veronica thought, Cecily was rude behind people's back so at least this was a slightly more honest way of operating. Barnaby had woken up during the Digby drama to eat three bowls of Mrs Hardman's stew, read a couple of newspapers, and give a very short statement to the police. He was now staring at his wife, looking rather more focused than usual.

Florence opened her eyes.

'I think it's great that Magnus has started looking for jobs, Cecily,' she said, her voice full of exhaustion. 'Don't you think we should all encourage him, rather than putting him off?'

Cecily gave a tiny snort. It was almost imperceptible, but Sister Veronica's sharp ears heard it.

Florence sighed, and her gaze wandered to a photo of her and Giles hanging on the wall. They looked happy in it, Sister Veronica thought, at some party or other. Their cheeks were flushed, they had wine glasses in their hands, and Giles had his arm round his wife. A moment of pleasure captured forever.

'I really can't believe he's gone,' she said, her voice becoming thick with emotion. 'I just can't seem to digest that he's never going to walk in to the room again, never going to go outside to clean his beloved cars anymore. His personality was so big, his absence seems to have left a physical hole in the house. And we were together for so many years.'

Cecily muttered something under her breath.

'What was that, Cecily?' Florence turned to her. 'I didn't quite catch it.'

'My words were...' Cecily said with a ruthless smile. 'Why do you miss him so much? It's not like you had a great marriage.'

'Now that's *enough*, Cecily.' Barnaby sat forward. 'I think you might need to go to bed soon. You've had quite enough to drink this evening.' *Gosh*, Sister Veronica thought. *So Barnaby is more observant than he appears to be. Happy to coast along most of the time, but says something when he thinks it's important. Good for him.*

'Her and me both,' Rufus said, holding his near empty glass in the air. He'd worked his way through the best part of a bottle of sweet sherry while the rest of them were drinking hot chocolate, Sister Veronica had noticed. But what was interesting was that Araminta hadn't touched a drop of alcohol since she'd got home. She'd been sitting curled up in an armchair since the police had left, staring into the middle distance, as though she was thinking about something very hard. Every now and again she rubbed the side of her head. *Must have hit it quite hard on her way down the stairs*, Sister Veronica thought. *That will smart for a good few days if you ask me.*

'I'm not going to bed, Barnaby, you silly man,' Cecily said with a laugh. 'I'm only just getting started. For the first time in days I'm actually having fun. You have your wine cellar to thank for that,' she said, turning to Florence, who narrowed her eyes at her sister-in-law.

'My wine cellar is now closed for the evening,' Florence said, a sharpness in her tone. 'And my marriage was a good one, thank you, Cecily. What gives you the right to judge it now, anyway?'

'Oh, just the fact that I knew Giles a lot better than you did,' Cecily said, a breeziness in her words. *She really is enjoying herself*, Sister Veronica thought. *Obnoxious woman.* 'Giles and I ended up, ah, spending a lot of time together over the years, Florence. Usually when you'd taken to your bed with some little problem or other.'

'*Shut up*, Mummy,' Araminta said, coming to suddenly. 'I think you've said enough now. Leave poor Auntie Florence alone. You're drunk, and you're saying things you don't mean.' She touched the side of her head, wincing.

'Bit like how you behave usually, isn't it, darling?' Cecily turned to her daughter. 'Drinking like a fish and saying and doing exactly what you feel.' She giggled. 'It is fun, I must say, I should do it more often.'

'I've decided to stop drinking alcohol altogether actually,' Araminta said. 'That's what I've been thinking about all evening. I don't want to get into that state anymore. Seeing how you are now, Mummy, just cements my decision. It's awful to look at. It's embarrassing. Listen everybody.' She looked round. 'I'm so sorry if I've been a pain to be with over the last few days. I'm sorry about falling down the stairs. I'm so ashamed about that. In fact, I've done quite a few things recently that I'm not proud of. My constant headache will be a reminder not to drink for now. It's going to be hard but I'll get there.'

Rufus shot her a warning look, as though trying to tell her not to say any more about whatever those things she wasn't proud of were. *How curious*, Sister Veronica thought. *Surely Araminta hasn't done anything so bad she can't share it with her family?* She gave her a warm smile.

'Good for you, Araminta,' Florence said, not taking her eyes from Cecily. 'That's a very brave decision. I must say, you and Magnus have really impressed me this evening.'

'Oh God.' Cecily snorted loudly. 'It's turning into an AA meeting.'

'Cecily,' Florence said, sitting up and shifting the blanket off her knees. 'I take it from what you said a few seconds ago that you are implying you and Giles had an affair behind my back?'

'Don't do this now, Florence,' Sister Veronica said, leaning forwards. 'Let's talk about it in the morning when she's sobered up a bit. Enough has gone on for one day, don't you think?'

'I need to know, V,' Florence said. 'Now that she's brought it up, I need to hear the truth.'

'Of *course* we had an affair.' Cecily waved her mug around. 'It wasn't like you were available for him, was it, Florence? Always busy with Magnus or suffering a migraine or a bout of depression. The man had needs, and I understood them. Don't worry, he ended it four years ago, we weren't still together when he died.'

Florence stood up and walked over to stand in front of Cecily.

'You utter bitch,' she said quietly. With one swift movement she threw the contents of her steaming mug of hot chocolate into Cecily's face, then turned and walked out of the room.

27

'Did you know about this, Daddy?' Araminta rushed over to give him a hug, ignoring her mother's anguished screams. *The drink had still been very hot,* Sister Veronica thought. *No doubt Cecily's face was scalded. Not that anyone particularly cared. Although she did really, she couldn't pretend otherwise – dash her compassionate disposition. She would go and tend to Cecily later, make sure she wasn't actually burnt.* Lucie let out a string of expletives in her mother's direction, and went to join her sister.

'Oh yes, darling, I've known for years.' Barnaby patted Araminta's back, not looking at his wife. 'Giles did me a favour, in fact. Took your mother off my hands for a good while. She's always been such hard work, always so demanding, never satisfied with her life. When she and him were at it I actually got some peace. You don't need to feel sorry for me.'

Sister Veronica shook her head and stood up. Just when she thought no other dramas could possibly occur that evening. She placed her mug down on the coffee table and went in search of her cousin.

Florence turned out to be slumped over the kitchen counter.

'I'm so stupid, V,' she whispered, when Sister Veronica put

her arm round her. 'Now I think about it, it all makes sense. There were so many little things that perhaps I chose to ignore. Like Giles offering to drive Cecily home when she'd been to stay. He never did that with anyone else. Maybe I've subconsciously known all the time, but just ignored it.'

'Perhaps,' Sister Veronica said with a sigh. 'But it doesn't change the good times you and Giles had together. Always remember that. It seems he was just a weak man in one respect.'

'He was a weak man in many ways, V,' Florence said. 'But my way of dealing with my lot in life was to think highly of him. It was a choice I made. Either be unhappy, and constantly be irritated and frustrated with his shortcomings, or live in blind and blissful ignorance.'

'And that was an understandable coping mechanism.' Sister Veronica rubbed her cousin's back. 'But you don't need to do that anymore, Flo. You have a chance to concentrate on yourself now. When all this awful stress and horror that's going on at the moment has finally finished, you can take time to do the things that make *you* happy, without worrying about anyone else for a while.'

'I've just had a thought, V,' Florence said, standing up straight. 'Cecily said that the relationship between her and Giles finished four years ago, didn't she? That he was the one who ended it?'

Sister Veronica nodded.

'Well, what if she was bitter about it being over?' Florence said. 'She's an incredibly bitter woman at the best of times, always hinting that she would do better at running Chalfield Hall than me. Oh yes, I notice all her little comments, I've just been choosing to ignore most of them. What if she was hoping Giles would chuck me out, so she could move in and take my place? Maybe it was her who poisoned Giles as revenge?' Her hands went to her mouth, as the awfulness of this motive and scenario hit her.

'Let's not jump to any conclusions, Flo,' Sister Veronica said, trying to keep her voice calm. 'If I'm honest with you, I've noticed that several people may have had problems with Giles. Not just Cecily. We have to be very careful before we go around accusing anyone to their face.'

'Several people?' Florence said. 'Like who?'

Sister Veronica explained about the argument she'd overheard between Giles and Rufus the night of his death. How they'd come out to talk just after dinner, and she'd overheard them from her place in the hall. She admitted she'd also listened to Cecily's remarks about Giles and Florence being house-hoggers, and had wondered about her apparent obsession with Chalfield Hall – all explained since her admission about her affair with Giles. She described what Romilly had said to her about Magnus being signed off with stress after working for his father, about Romilly's brother Steven being fired by Giles for apparently being too late for work in the mornings, and what Wilfred had said about overhearing his mother, father and uncle talking about going to a lawyer with the hope of bringing some sort of charges against him. Florence listened, open-mouthed.

'Why are you only telling me all this now, V?' she said, her eyes wide.

'I've been trying to get things straight in my own mind, Flo,' Sister Veronica said, her brow crinkling. 'And you've had enough to deal with. Your husband has just died – probably murdered. I didn't want to add to your worries until I had thought things through and maybe discovered a little more.' *No point telling Flo I had to consider whether she herself had a hand in Giles' death*, she thought. *No, that wouldn't be helpful to anyone at this stage, and would probably drive a terrible wedge between us.*

Florence nodded, seeming to accept this is a viable explanation.

'Mrs Hardman said something strange to me earlier, actually,' Florence said, looking thoughtful. 'You just reminded me about it, when you said about Giles upsetting people. I forgot about it, what with all that happened with Digby...'

'What was it?' Sister Veronica said.

'Well,' Florence said. 'It was when you were upstairs checking the rooms, and I'd come downstairs to do the same. I didn't really want to talk to Mrs Hardman, but she was insistent, and there was a look in her eyes that made me stop and listen. She said that a week or two before you all arrived here for Christmas, she went to the study to clean it, and found Giles there, staring at some sort of online banking page. She said he was tearing at his hair, and making some sort of awful groaning sound, that he was obviously upset about something. As he hadn't realised she was there, Mrs Hardman said she decided to tiptoe away, wanting to mind her own business, and hadn't thought anything more about it. That's until he died, that is.'

'I see.' Sister Veronica straightened up. 'Gosh, that puts an interesting new slant on things, Flo. I mean, if there was something terribly wrong in Giles' business, let's say, would he have been stressed enough to take his own life? Poison himself? We've been thinking there's a murderer among us all this time – not including Ophelia – but what if Giles did it to himself?'

Florence shook her head.

'I just can't see him doing that, V,' she said. 'It's not that I'm being delusional or anything, not wanting him to have committed suicide. If I genuinely thought he had it in him to do it, I'd say so. But my husband was almost stubbornly alive, if you know what I mean. He had such a drive and will to live, it shone out of him. Admittedly, I've recently found out that his idea of 'living' was much more immoral than mine, but even so. And he very rarely took responsibility for anything. He couldn't, he had a pathological need to blame others if things went wrong. If something awful had happened at work, I think he would have blamed someone else, not himself, for whatever it was.'

Sister Veronica nodded.

'I think you might be right,' she said. 'Did he ever give you any impression that something was wrong? That he might be worrying about money or anything else?'

'No,' Florence said. 'Never. In fact, he kept saying business was booming, that the profits from Beresford's Breaded Wonders were flowing in. I really never had any reason to suspect this wasn't true, what with Giles telling me to pick out a new kitchen, and new colours for the dining room. He acted as though his business was raking profits in, and he was being extremely free with his money. Always was, in fact. Looking back, now that I know what I do, maybe there were some signs I should have picked up on. Or perhaps I should have shown a greater interest in his work, and checked the books sometimes. But I'd never been involved in it like that before, do you know what I mean? Beresford's Breaded Wonders was always his territory.'

'I think,' Sister Veronica said, 'that we need to have a look at his bank accounts, Flo. If Mrs Hardman specifically mentioned an online banking page, then that's where we need to look next. We are very likely to discover things from that, by the sounds of it, that may be painful for you to know but necessary to absorb in order to understand what on earth is going on in this house. Do you know his password for his laptop?'

'Not officially,' Florence said, standing up. 'But I have a good idea what it might be. Come with me.'

28

'Ah there you are, Auntie Florence.' Lucie was coming down the corridor as they exited the kitchen. She gave a big, almost forced smile. 'I, um, don't suppose you have a minute for a quick chat? I know it's been an awful day, and I wouldn't ask if this wasn't urgent, but there's something I've been wanting to talk to you about.'

'I'm sorry, my dear, but I'm afraid that whatever it is going to have to wait.' Florence gave her niece's shoulder a quick pat as she circumnavigated her. 'Something's come up that's critically important, and V and I are going to have to shut ourselves in the study for a while. We'll make time to talk tomorrow, Lucie, if we don't get a chance tonight, I promise.' Sister Veronica watched Lucie's face drop into a mask of worry and disappointment. *What can the girl want to talk to Flo about that's so important?* she wondered. *Well, it will unfortunately have to be put on hold for a little bit longer, whatever it is.*

Minutes later, she was shutting the study door, as Florence settled herself in the comfortable, leather-bound swivel chair in front of Giles' still open laptop. It smelt of Giles in the room, Sister Veronica noticed. Perhaps it was a lingering smell of aftershave, or the amount of expensive leather products in there – she always associated a leathery smell with him for some reason. He was definitely around, an imprint of him still present at Chalfield Hall. She wondered if her cousin had noticed. Florence wasn't showing any signs of being upset by it, if indeed she had noticed. Perhaps finding out about Cecily and her husband's affair had changed her feelings for him. Sister Veronica watched as her cousin plugged in the charging lead, and waited for the machine to whir into life.

While she was waiting for Flo to get the whole thing up and running, she busied herself looking at the family photos arrayed all over the wall. There were plenty of Florence, Giles and Magnus, some of Wilfred and Coco as young tots, and a couple when they were older. Only one of Cecily and Barnaby looking very stiff and regal, and a couple of Lucie and Araminta that must have been taken when they were teenagers. *Ah*, she thought. *There's good old Tarquin, Florence's youngest brother, and his wife Marina. Such a shame that awful cancer got hold of him so quickly a few years ago.* Marina, she suspected, had died of a broken heart very soon afterwards. It happened sometimes – in her experience – when two people were very close; they sometimes departed the earth almost at the same time, but for very different reasons, almost as though their life purposes had been intertwined, and would be in heaven as on earth. *Poor Ophelia*, she thought, *losing both her parents in such a short space of time. That must have been hard.* She stopped, a photo of a young, serious girl catching her eye.

'Is that Ophelia?' she said.

'What?' Florence said, turning round. 'Oh yes, it is. She must have been about seven in that one. Such a solemn child. I always worried about her, wondered if she was a bit bored growing up in that big house with just Tarquin and Marina for company. They were so pleased when they adopted her, I remember. They were older then, had been trying for a child for years but with no luck. It was affecting them both quite badly, getting them down. Then suddenly, one day, Marina phoned me to say they'd been given the chance to have a beautiful baby girl come to live with them. It must have been through an adoption agency or something, they never said, but it must have been, mustn't it? And I never knew who Ophelia's parents were, they never told me and I never asked. They were private people, weren't they, who liked to keep themselves to themselves?'

Sister Veronica nodded.

'Anyway.' Florence turned back round to face the screen. 'They loved Ophelia very much in their own way, and always did the best for her that they could. I just worried a bit that they were sort of old-fashioned, not really the huggy types, if you know what I mean? A bit stuffy. Tarquin was never like that as a boy, he changed when he hit thirty, became all serious and conservative for some reason. It would have been wonderful if Ophelia had had a brother or a sister to run around with, but, of course, that was never possible. She was always an only child.'

'Quite,' Sister Veronica agreed, looking at the girl in the photo's deep-set eyes. 'I hardly want to mention it, but it seems more than a coincidence that Digby fell over the railing and died shortly after Ophelia went upstairs. I don't think any of us will blame her if she did do it, the man was evil, an abuser who used her mistake to keep her in a life of constant punishment and misery. But still, the police will conduct their investigations. I do hope they go easy on her. It's so strange, with her looking increasingly radiant since his death, but knowing she may well have pushed him. I hardly know what to say to her anymore. But we all saw how he treated her, and we'll all speak up if need be.'

'Exactly,' Florence said, a firmness in her voice. 'It was a hideous thing that happened, I mean a death like that is tragic and awful, whoever the person is. But I noticed how much calmer she seems already, this evening, and like you said – almost radiant. She's been set free, and I'll protect her from any comeuppance with every bone in my body. The poor girl has been through enough. She and Sam both deserve to have a shot at a new life now.'

'Hear hear,' Sister Veronica said, her eyes going to the laptop as movement on the screen caught her attention. She watched, as a page appeared, asking for the username and password to be entered.

'Giles was a fantastic businessman,' Florence said. 'Well, at least I thought he was – turns out the truth is a bit different. One thing he definitely wasn't, though, was a technological whiz. I've heard him talking on the phone several times over the last few years, setting up different accounts for one thing and another. When it came time for whoever it was to ask him for a password, he always gave the same answer.'

'And what was it?' Sister Veronica said.

'He always spelt out 28th April 1901,' Florence said. 'It was his mother's date of birth.'

She leant forward and tapped Giles' email address into the username box, and his mother's date of birth into the one that said password. Giles' home screen immediately whooshed into life, sporting a colourful array of app icons.

Sister Veronica bent down to have a good look at them.

'Gracious, there are a lot of them,' she said. 'Is one of these connected with his bank?'

'Probably.' Florence scanned the screen. 'I have access to our joint account, so we don't need to look at that one. I know how much is in there, I check it fairly regularly. As far as I know, in terms of other accounts, Giles just had a business bank one with Royal Swan. Ah, look, there we go.' She clicked on an image of a black-and-white swan and a few seconds later a banking page appeared in front of them. They both stared at it, trying to take in and make sense of the lists of numbers in front of them.

'But, this can't be right, V?' Florence said, swivelling round to face her, her eyes wide. 'I'm probably not reading it correctly, but to me it seems as though this is saying Giles' business account has no money in it at all. In fact, it seems to be saying that Beresford's Breaded Wonders is overdrawn by nearly a million pounds.'

29

Both women were too engrossed in the catastrophic information in front of them to notice soft footsteps padding away from the study door.

Lucie, her mind racing and tears falling from her eyes, made her way blindly up to the bedroom she'd been sharing with Neil. She grabbed her phone and called him. He answered straight away.

'Hi, Luce, sorry I was just about to text you. We've just arrived home,' he said.

'Oh, Neil.' Big sobs full of defeat overtook her. 'You were right, I should have just come back with you and the boys.'

'Why?' Neil said, his voice suddenly concerned. 'Are you all right, Luce? What's happened?'

'Auntie Florence doesn't have any money,' Lucie said through her tears. 'She can't lend me any. I'm going to have to resign from my PhD.'

'How do you know, have you just been talking to her?' Neil said.

'I overheard her and Sister Veronica chatting. Auntie Florence was saying that there's absolutely no money in Giles' business anymore. In fact, it's in debt for nearly a million pounds.' Lucie was finding it hard to get the words out.

'What?' Neil's tone was shocked. 'But how can that be? Giles was always boasting about how well he was doing.' He sighed. 'Look, Luce, just come home and we can talk about everything. We'll work something out.'

'I really thought I'd be able to finish my studies, Neil.' Lucie's voice was rising. 'I so wanted to make a difference in the world and do something that mattered, something I could use to help women and men who've been abused. But now I'm going to have to go back to doing a meaningless job that doesn't help anyone.'

'It helps *us*, Lucie,' Neil said slowly. 'If you can work and bring some money in each month, it will help Nathan and Ryan continue at rugby, and me and you pay the bills. Do you see that?'

'Yes, of course I do,' Lucie said, her tone changing from distraught to angry. 'I was just trying to combine getting an even better job in the future with something I feel passionately about. I actually thought that would set a good example to the boys, teach them that they can do anything in life if they set their minds to it, do something they really care about. But it doesn't matter anymore, Neil. I'll come home first thing tomorrow and I'll phone the university after Christmas and resign. I'll get a stupid mind-numbing job just to bring some money in, and try and forget about the dream qualification I nearly gained. There. Happy now?'

'No,' Neil said. 'Of course I'm not happy. I love you, Luce, and I've been trying to support you as much as I can for months, only you're too busy navel-gazing to see that. I don't want to see you upset. But equally, I don't want us all to lose this house and become homeless.'

'Okay, Neil,' Lucie said, wiping her eyes. 'I'm sorry, I don't mean to take this all out on you, I was just so sure Auntie

Florence would be able help me, maybe lend me some money that, of course, I'd pay back to her when I could. Anyway, it doesn't matter now. Listen, I'm going to have a drink. I'll see you tomorrow. Love you.'

She ended the call and threw her phone hard on the bed. Everything was fucked up. Why did Uncle Giles' business account have to be empty, for God's sake? He and Auntie Florence always appeared to have loads of money; the nice cars, plentiful food, Giles' frequent boasts about how well his business was doing. And they'd just redecorated the house, hadn't they? If there were no profits from his business, Beresford's Breaded Wonders, in his account, then what the bloody hell had happened to them?

30

It's Christmas Eve, Sister Veronica thought, opening her eyes. For a moment, a thrill of childish excitement ran through her. She always loved this time of year, her parents had been superb at creating a festive atmosphere when she was young – purposefully taking time out from their busy farming life to make things special. She remembered how they'd decorated the tree together, and hung holly and mistletoe around the house. She could almost feel the anticipation of long-ago Christmas Eve nights, when little Veronica had gazed out of her bedroom window wondering if she'd see Father Christmas and his reindeer whizzing through the sky. She'd wake up while it was still dark and the small but tightly packed stocking would be waiting at the end of her bed, filled with modest but much-loved goodies. But memories of the horrific happenings of the previous two days slowly plopped into her mind like heavy stones. Soon, she was feeling weighed down with all the tragedy and secrecy at Chalfield Hall, her Christmassy rush of goodwill and nostalgia vanishing almost as soon as it had arrived.

By the time she'd washed and dressed and arrived downstairs, just Ophelia and Sam were sitting at the kitchen counter, a plate of half-eaten toast triangles next to the little boy. It was the first time she'd seen Ophelia in casual clothes, jeans and a jumper, rather than the beautiful but formal tailored suits she seemed to favour.

'Lucie gave them to me,' Ophelia said with a smile, noticing the nun's gaze. 'She said they were too small for her now, and wondered if I'd like them. It's nice of her, I don't own any jeans.'

Sister Veronica nodded and smiled, then turned towards the sideboard. The smell of coffee in the room and the sight of several empty mugs by the sink suggested that she was one of the last to rise that day. Dash, that was unlike her. If she wasn't careful she'd become as slovenly as Maud and start lying in bed till noon. She could imagine what Mother Superior would have to say about that sort of carry-on back at the convent. She'd never put up with it, she'd have any nun who tried it up and in chapel for extra prayers within seconds.

She busied herself, filling up the kettle and turning it on, sourcing a clean mug and plate and making herself two slices of toast, all the while wondering whether she should address Digby's demise with Ophelia. Should she subtly bring up the notion that it would be understandable if an abused woman had harmed the man who'd hurt her for so many years? Probably best not at the moment, she concluded, as she extracted the butter and jam from the fridge. Not while the little boy's present, at any rate. He shouldn't have to listen to any more negativity, little lamb. Especially where his mother and father were concerned.

She'd just placed her breakfast on top of the counter and herself on a bar stool, when Maud came in. Glancing at the clock, Sister Veronica saw it was half past nine.

'Morning, Maud,' she said with a smile. 'Up early today?'

'I didn't sleep very well at all last night, Sister,' Maud said. Her eyes, on closer inspection, did look rather puffy and tired,

Sister Veronica realised. Was there also a certain greyness to her skin, or was she imagining it?

'Well, no surprises there,' Sister Veronica said, with a grimace. 'The last two days have been particularly frightful for everyone, haven't they? Poor Giles, such an unexpected collapse. And what happened with Digby. Well, it's too awful to talk about – I don't think I'll ever forget the sight of him on the hall floor. It was probably the stress of all that which kept you awake, I imagine.'

'Yes, most likely,' Maud mumbled, walking round her and reaching for the coffee. 'Awful things do keep happening this Christmas, don't they? I expect it's that. I usually sleep quite well.'

'Oh before I forget,' Ophelia said, turning. 'The hospital just rang for you, Maud. I tried looking for you but you weren't in your room. They said you need to phone them back urgently, they left a number, I wrote it down on the pad by the house phone.'

'Oh.' Maud looked up. 'Thanks, Ophelia. Probably about my indigestion. It's been terrible recently, I've had to have some tests done.'

Sister Veronica watched her, saying nothing. *No hospital would phone on Christmas Eve if the problem was just about indigestion*, she thought. *I hope Maud isn't ill. Still, if she wants to keep the real reason about the call private then that's up to her, I suppose. Not my place to pry.*

'Ah, morning everyone.' Florence came into the kitchen. 'V, I've just been on the phone with my accountant. Are you free for a minute?'

'Yes.' Sister Veronica looked longingly at her heavily buttered toast, now slathered with jam. Oh well, she could always make some fresh slices after Florence had finished whatever she had to say. She got up and followed her cousin into the hall.

'V, it's bad,' Florence said, stopping next to the Christmas tree. 'I sent everything to my accountant early this morning, all of Giles' business accounts, and our own personal one. He was able to tell quite quickly what's been going on.'

'What, Flo?' Sister Veronica said, alarmed by her cousin's wide eyes, a look of shock in them.

'It seems my husband's business, Beresford's Breaded Wonders, hasn't been doing very well after all,' Florence said. 'In fact, that's an understatement. For the last few years, the profits have fallen dramatically. I'm not sure why; maybe the public have gone off fish fingers – I must say, I can't blame them if they have, I've personally had quite enough of them to last me a lifetime.'

'Oh,' Sister Veronica said. 'Then how on earth did Giles have enough money to keep buying cars and to do up the house?'

'Exactly,' Florence said, her eyes narrowing. 'The stupid man was siphoning off what money there was left in the business into our joint bank account. I saw the transfers, and presumed he was just paying himself a monthly wage like usual. But it seems he was actually taking money that wasn't his, that should have been used to pay the wages of his workers. And some of it belonged to the shareholders in the business. I'm one of them, so are many members of the family, who – incidentally – are going to be livid when they find out about all this. Giles actually went so far with his scheme that his business is now massively in debt. Ridiculous, foolish man that he was.'

'Flo,' Sister Veronica said slowly. 'I'm just thinking about what you just said, that you and other members of the family are shareholders in Beresford's Breaded Wonders, and that they will be furious when they find out what Giles was up to. But what if one or more of them already knew about what Giles was up to?

What if that's the reason behind the poison pen letters, and even his death – that they found out and were trying to get him to stop taking all the money?'

'Crikey, you're right.' Florence reached out to the wall to steady herself. 'That makes sense really, doesn't it? Can't blame them for the poison pen letters, if that's what they were about. Although I'd rather that whoever it was had come and just told me about it, face to face. But murdering him for it? That's too far, that's beyond reasonable anger. It's inexcusable.'

'Yes,' Sister Veronica said, giving a heavy sigh. 'Although unfortunately, people don't always think rationally when they're pushed beyond a certain point, particularly where money is concerned. And especially when it comes to family matters, it seems.' Something white that was lying near the front door caught her attention.

'Oh no, Flo, I think you might have received another one of those dratted letters,' she said, walking over and bending down to pick it up. 'When on earth did this arrive?' She turned it over to read the name on the front, but the sight of what she saw made her gasp and almost drop it.

'What is it, V?' Florence hurried over to her.

They both stared at the name inscribed on the front of the envelope in capital letters: SISTER VERONICA.

31

Maud settled back into the biggest armchair in the living room, her pile of pink knitting on her knee. For some reason she wasn't getting very far with it that day. It was a nuisance that the hospital had rung Chalfield Hall's home telephone instead of her mobile – which to be fair was probably off or on silent – it usually was – she'd never been that keen on new-fangled technology. Now people might suspect she was poorly, which was a little wearing. She lied about her illness to keep her business private and had no intention of truthfully answering any inquisitive, well-meaning questions from anyone. She'd had to give her doctor the contact details of where she'd be staying over the Christmas period as a precaution, of course, but she never thought they'd actually phone her there. Yes, her prognosis was grim, but it had been good to spend time with close family without them knowing and fussing around and making her feel like an invalid. She knew this would be the last Christmas she ever spent with the people she cared about. And there were currently people she cared about at Chalfield much more than others. Much, *much* more.

Maud had decided to make the best of life in the most enjoyable way she could a long time ago. She hadn't had the best childhood in the world, and things had happened before she'd left home that had scarred her so deeply she'd always had to carry the wounds with her, unspoken about but not forgotten, and impossible to fully shake off. She knew they'd shaped her, made her the private, insular person she was today, but that's just how it was, how it had to be. She had soon realised that the most pleasant way for her to cope with life and its demands was to live vividly inside her head, in a way distancing herself from external reality. Things were less painful that way. Maud was an introvert, isn't that what people called those like her nowadays? She had a good idea that to the outside world she came across as remote and cut off, not really ever joining in properly with things, and always hovering in the background at family events. But she suspected that she was a lot more intelligent than anyone ever realised. And it was fine with her that that was her own little secret, because inside her head she'd become entirely self-sufficient, and she didn't need people properly getting to know her, and butting in to her protected inner world.

She did, however, enjoy being with those she loved, more as an observer than a participant. Just knowing they were alive and well was enough for her; that they would go on – strong and healthy – long after she was dead and buried. That's really why she'd accepted Florence's invitation to Chalfield Hall that Christmas. She'd been surprised to receive it, of course, had wondered why Florence had invited her – it wasn't like the two of them had ever been that close, it had been a long while since she'd last seen the woman. But she'd soon realised the opportunity that it would bring her, and it was one she couldn't afford to miss. In her own way, just spending time near her relatives was her goodbye to them. She was doing it quietly, and only she knew what was in store for her in a few months: death.

There was, however, one last thing Maud needed to do before she was ready to say goodbye to the world. And it would be done soon. She picked up her needles and began to knit.

32

'Oh, V, what does it say?' Florence peered at the sheet of paper in Sister Veronica's hands.

'It just says, "Stop interfering. You have been warned",' Sister Veronica said. 'But look, Flo, doesn't the writing look a bit different to the letters you've been getting?'

Florence leaned forwards and stared.

'I'm not sure,' she said slowly. 'Bring it upstairs and we can compare them.'

Minutes later, Sister Veronica was sitting on Florence's bed, watching her cousin retrieve a wooden box from her bureau before unlocking it with a small key she took out from under a vase. Everything in the room was beautiful, she noticed, in a heavy, old kind of way. Much of the furniture must have been left over from mad old Henrietta's time, and would no doubt be passed down to each family member as they took the place over when the time came. Bringing the pile of letters from inside it to the bed, Florence sat down, and the pair of them stared from Sister Veronica's letter to several of Florence's.

'Yes,' Florence said, after a while. 'You're right, V, you must be much more observant than me. Now that I see them together, the style of the writing is obviously different. Whoever wrote mine has looser handwriting, while yours is written tightly with more control.'

'Absolutely.' Sister Veronica nodded. 'Do you recognise either types? Remind you of the writing in any letters or cards you've received, particularly from family?'

Florence exhaled, staring from one to the other.

'It's so hard to tell, isn't it?' she said. 'I mean, whoever wrote the letters obviously didn't want to be discovered, so they've put some effort into trying to just write in plain capital letters. But even so you can tell that yours and mine are produced by different hands. I just don't know who they belong to.'

Sister Veronica was about to reply, when raised voices caught her attention.

'Listen,' she said, putting her hand on Florence's arm. They sat in silence for a minute. The voices got louder. They clearly belonged to a man and a woman.

'That sounds like Araminta and Rufus,' Florence said in a low voice, her brow furrowing. 'Which is unusual, because those two rarely argue. Drink together? Yes, from dusk till dawn. But fight? Hardly ever, not that I've seen, anyway.'

Sister Veronica folded her letter, placed it on the bed, and stood up. She crept over to the door and quietly, slowly opened it.

'No, Minty,' they could hear Rufus saying. There was an edge of desperation in his voice. 'No, you can't. You really *can't*. Listen to what I'm saying, Minty. If you tell everyone, it will be the end of us, trust me.'

'I don't care,' Araminta said. *She's sounding strong*, Sister Veronica thought. *Not drunk at all, her speech is clear and precise. Good for her.* 'I've had enough of the whole stupid thing. It was a terrible idea, I should never have gone along with it. In fact, I've been saying yes to you when I meant no for a long time now. I thought I was going to die the other day, Rufie, when I came to in the ambulance, and you just seemed to think it was funny. All you did was laugh about me falling down the stairs. "Oh don't worry about Minty, she'll be fine, she always does this." But I wasn't fine, and I'm not now. But one thing I have realised – ever since I was thinking about things in the hospital – is that I don't want to live like this anymore.'

'What do you mean, live like this?' Rufus said.

'Dishonestly and pathetically,' Araminta said. 'Meaning-lessly, just drinking ourselves to death.'

'Oh God, Minty, why are you being so *boring* all of a sudden?' There was an edge of irritation in Rufus' voice. 'One thing I've always loved about you is that you're a party girl through and through. Always up for a good time, ready to have fun when the stuffy people around us are being dull and sensible. Don't change, for God's sake.'

'I've been "changed" inside for a while now, Rufus,' Araminta said. 'I just didn't have the guts to tell you, or show you, that I wanted more out of life. I just went along with you and your wishes like usual, because I love you, and because I've been weak. But I've got enough strength in me now to do what's best for *me*.'

'You'll ruin yourself, if you think you can act like Pollyanna and just come clean to everyone.' Sister Veronica could hear movement now, as though someone was walking into the corridor. 'Everyone will hate us, they won't understand,' Rufus was saying. 'We'll be cut out of the will. I'm telling you, Minty, if you go through with this you'll regret it for the rest of your life. And so will I. You won't just destroy your own reputation, you'll wreck mine too.' A door slammed, and footsteps pounded down the landing. Sister Veronica quickly pushed her cousin's door with her hand and it swung to quietly, nearly closing but not quite. She held her breath, and it looked as though Florence was doing the same. The footsteps – Rufus' by the heavy sound of them – passed by without slowing down. She heard him jogging down the stairs, and seconds later the front door slammed.

Florence looked at her.

'Well!' she said. 'What on earth have those two been up to?'

33

'Hello, Mrs Hardman,' Maud said, entering the kitchen. 'What treats have you got in store for us for this lunchtime?'

'Ah, Maud.' Mrs Hardman glanced round briefly. 'Today's lunch will be prune-and-apple stuffed pork belly with roast fennel. I'm making a separate, smaller mushroom and chestnut Wellington for Lucie, what with her being vegetarian and everything.' She turned back, slicing up a large apple with dexterity.

'Ooh, how delicious,' Maud said, walking over. 'Do you mind if I help?' She'd been offering to help the woman since arriving at Chalfield Hall, there was no reason why she should repel her offer now. It was a lot of work feeding so many people every day and the housekeeper always seemed glad to have an extra pair of hands in the kitchen. None of the others ever offered their services to her, not even the nun, which wasn't very charitable in her opinion.

'No,' Mrs Hardman said shortly. 'I don't mind. There's some pastry in the fridge that needs rolling. You can start with that if you like. Just take it out of the bowl and sprinkle some flour on the counter. Then after that you can chop the mushrooms.'

'Will do,' Maud said. *Excellent*, she thought, going over to open the refrigerator door. *Everything is running so smoothly. It's almost like my plan is meant to be.*

34

'Auntie Florence?' Araminta said. She stopped and took a deep breath. 'Could I possibly talk to you about something?'

'Yes, of course, dear.' Florence looked up. She and Sister Veronica had made themselves comfortable in the living room, ostensibly to read the papers but really to be accessible and available should Araminta want to talk to them, which clearly she did.

'Would you like me to go, Araminta?' Sister Veronica said. 'I totally understand if you'd rather chat to your aunt without me here?'

'No.' Araminta shook her head. 'Stay, Sister. You'll only find out anyway, so you may as well hear what I have to say right now.'

Sister Veronica nodded, and settled back into the sofa.

Araminta, perching awkwardly on the edge of an armchair, looked down at her hands. Then her eyes flitted very briefly to the drinks cabinet, a pang of hunger – desperation – in them, before she shook her head and stared back down again.

'Auntie Florence, there's no easy way to talk about this,' she said. She stopped for a minute and sighed. 'Rufus and I have done something awful, and I feel so ashamed about it.' Fat tears began falling down her cheeks. Sister Veronica reached over to the shelf, picked up the box of tissues, and passed it to her.

'Take your time, dear,' Florence said, with a kind smile.

Araminta exhaled. She looked up at her aunt.

'You've probably been finding rather nasty notes on your doormat every now and again,' she said, her face crumpling.

'Yes, Araminta, I have,' Florence said, her smile disappearing. 'They've been causing me a huge amount of anxiety over the last year. I've become quite ill with it.'

'I'm so sorry,' Araminta whispered, looking down again, her tears wetting her hands.

'So it was you and Rufus who were behind these letters, I take it?' Sister Veronica said. Araminta looked up at her and nodded. 'I think you should do your aunt the courtesy of explaining what on earth possessed you to send such vile notes to her, don't you?'

Araminta nodded again.

'It was Rufus' idea,' she said, her words coming out fast. 'He thought of doing it almost a year ago, after visiting Uncle Giles at the Beresford's Breaded Wonders factory. Rufie had just bought some more shares in the business and wanted to have a look round, to see how everything was going. He said that he'd been left alone in the study there for a while, as one of the workers had come to complain about some problem or other, and Uncle Giles had gone off with him to try and sort it out. While he was waiting, Rufus saw some documents on Giles' desk that caught his eye. When he looked closer, he saw that Giles' business – that Rufus has thousands of shares in, literally tens of thousands – was basically failing. I'm so sorry to tell you this, Auntie Florence, I'm not sure if you know about it?'

'Yes, I know,' Florence said quietly. 'Go on, Araminta.'

'Rufus also saw what he believed was evidence showing that Uncle Giles was embezzling the bit of income that *was* coming into the business,' Araminta said. 'He was so angry that night when he came home, ranting and raving around the house, saying that my uncle was a thief and a crook who would ruin us if something wasn't done about it.'

Florence nodded. Her emotions, so twisted and distorted because of everything that had happened, allowed a thump of compassion for Rufus to enter her heart. It must have been soul-destroying for him to discover that a man he trusted was deceiving him, robbing him.

'I said we should confront Uncle Giles, and tell him to give Rufie all the money back that he'd ploughed into Beresford's Breaded Wonders,' Araminta said. 'Rufus kept on and on trying to arrange a meeting with Giles, he called so many times, sent emails and text messages, but had no luck getting hold of him. In the end he just lost it, and said that as the nice, fair approach hadn't worked, he was going to have to take drastic measures.'

Florence sighed, nodding. Sister Veronica gave Araminta a small smile, willing her to carry on. It was good that the girl was getting this off her chest, being honest with her aunt. And in one way, she understood the desperation behind the notes, the feelings of anger and helplessness that Araminta and Rufus must have had, knowing Giles had lost their money. But she couldn't forgive them, not yet, not seeing how the despicable letters had affected Flo. But she would, of course, in time. She just needed to let the news sit with her for a bit, get acclimatised to it. It would be much easier to excuse Araminta, of course; she was showing genuine remorse. Rufus, on the other hand, was a different matter.

'All the time this was happening, Rufus' drinking was getting worse.' A fresh cascade of tears fell from Araminta's eyes. 'And so was mine, as I was trying to keep up with him. We've always drunk together in the evenings, you see. It's just the habit we fell into. Anyway, Rufie was desperate. He'd bought so many shares believing Uncle Giles' business was incredibly buoyant, and going from strength to strength, which is what we've always been told, haven't we?'

Florence nodded.

'It was Rufus' idea of giving us both a pension. The idea was that when we retired, we'd sell the shares and live comfortably off the proceeds. But now Rufie and I could see that we'd lost all that, and it was driving us both insane with worry. So Rufus came up with a plan. He said that you were bound to know about what Uncle Giles was doing, that he would never be able to transfer so much money into your personal account – he'd seen proof of this happening on some statement or other – without your knowledge and complicity. He said you were as bad as each other, and that you deserved what was coming to you, seeing as Uncle Giles wasn't prepared to meet him, man to man, to discuss everything.'

Florence took in a deep breath and exhaled slowly.

'Go on,' she said.

'So that's when Rufie said we were going to write you these letters, to try and intimidate you into doing the right thing, without you knowing who was sending them. He said Uncle Giles ruined him behind his back, so we were going to do the same to you, until you forced your husband to make things right. He said my uncle must be well aware that he – Rufie – was furious about it all, due to the amount of messages he'd left, telling him to sort the situation out. But that he probably wouldn't immediately realise who was sending the notes, given that so many of Uncle Giles' ex-workers and current employees were also livid with him about the late payments and the mistreatment.'

'I see,' Florence said slowly, nodding. 'I now have to tell you two things that may surprise you, Araminta. Firstly, I genuinely did not know Giles was doing this, that his business had gone under, and that he was siphoning off the remaining money into our personal account. You see, he'd always paid himself a wage from the profits, he'd done so for years. Because he kept telling me business was booming, I could see the money coming in each month but presumed it was just him paying himself the usual wage. And secondly.' Florence stared at her niece. 'I never told Giles about the notes you were posting through our door. Because I had no idea about the state of his business, I didn't know you were referring to that in your awful messages. I didn't want to worry him, he's never been very good in a crisis anyway – always went to pieces. I thought whoever was sending the messages meant us harm, and it was terrifying. Like I say, the notes have made me very ill over the last year. I just didn't understand who would be doing something so heinous to me.'

Araminta nodded, her face full of shame and despair.

'Auntie Florence, I'm just so, so sorry about all this,' she said, shaking her head. 'If I could take it back, I would. I just went along with it because Rufus was so insistent – I think he kind of wanted to punish you both. And to be honest, I haven't been all that sober for a long time, and that hasn't helped my decision-making.'

Florence regarded her niece for a long moment. Then she gave a small, sad smile.

'You have shown great courage in telling me this today,' she said. 'And I need to apologise to you, too, on behalf of my husband, for his actions, and for yours and Rufus' loss of money. If I'd even had the smallest inkling about what Giles was up to, I'd have done my utmost to put a stop to it.'

Sister Veronica leaned forwards.

'Why do you think he was doing it, Flo?' she said.

Florence gave a small shrug.

'I just think he couldn't bear to believe that our lifestyle would have to change,' she said. 'You know what Giles was like, always full of pomposity, he really enjoyed the status he felt that his business and this house brought him. Almost as though it made him better than other people, to have such money and possessions. I think a sort of madness must have come over him when he realised that – for whatever reason – his business had begun to fail. He did the only thing he could think of, deluding himself in the process, of keeping up the appearance of still being successful. The fact that he didn't even tell me about it shows how desperate he must have felt, how he just couldn't let go and sort the situation out sensibly. If he'd told me, we could have sold the house, paid his debts and employees, and started afresh in a smaller cottage somewhere. But the stupid man just kept everything to himself.'

She shook her head.

Araminta's brow furrowed.

'I thought you'd be furious with me when I told you,' she said to her aunt. 'Chuck Rufie and I out of Chalfield Hall immediately. And I wouldn't have blamed you if you had.'

Florence gave a smile tinged with bitterness.

'I am furious,' she said. 'But mainly with Giles. And I'm also cross with myself for not having been more involved, not picking up on any signs that might have been there. What you and Rufus did was a cowardly, vindictive act, Araminta, but it wasn't without provocation. Giles treated you both very badly. If he'd been honest to start with, none of this would have ever happened. So while you have put me through the most stressful year of my life with all your poison pen letters, I cannot solely blame the two of you for the situation. And I'm very grateful for your apology. It has healed some of the hurt inside me.'

Araminta jumped up and enveloped her aunt in an enormous hug.

'Thank you,' she said into Florence's shoulder. 'You really are an amazing lady, Auntie Florence.'

Well, Sister Veronica thought. *If Flo is big enough to forgive her niece, then so am I.*

An ear-shattering scream split the atmosphere in two.

'That sounds like Coco,' Florence said, her voice full of alarm. 'What on earth has happened to her now?'

35

Seconds later, they arrived in the study to find Magnus – sitting in the leather swivel chair, his laptop on the desk in front of him – turning round to stare at his daughter. His face looked different from the inert, blank expression she was used to, Sister Veronica thought. It had life in it, more colour. And it didn't look happy.

'No, Coco,' he said, his voice loud and firm. 'You can scream and shout at me as much as you want, but I have no plans to buy you a new car or give you my credit card for your endless online shopping until I see a big improvement in your behaviour. One that lasts more than a few hours.'

'I hate you!' Coco's voice was a scream. Her body was so tense it looked brittle, as though she could snap at any moment. 'You're a crap father, and now you're taking away my only enjoyment in life. I wish I was dead.' *Ah*, Sister Veronica thought. *So last night's brief reaction of listening to her father has worn off, I see. That's a shame, we're back to the drama and accusations. Maybe I better step in and see if I can reason with her.*

'Coco,' she said, stepping forward. 'Do you mind if I have a quick word?'

The girl spun round to look at her, her eyes wide and unhinged.

'I couldn't help noticing the drawings on the walls in your room when I was looking for your aunt last night,' Sister Veronica said. 'Did you do them?'

Coco gave the briefest of nods.

'They show exceptional talent,' Sister Veronica said, allowing an encouraging smile to spread across her face. 'I'm not just saying that, your use of tone and line is beautiful, as is your eye for composition. They really moved me, the emotion in them is rather remarkable.'

Coco's breathing slowed down a bit.

'No one else seems that interested in them,' she said.

'I am.' Florence leaned towards her. 'I've told you before how beautiful I think your work is, Coco, and how you should think about applying for a place at art college.'

'This is just an idea.' Sister Veronica flashed a glance at Magnus to see if he minded her talking to his daughter. He gave her a quick nod, that seemed to imply 'carry on'. 'I've noticed, since my arrival at Chalfield Hall, that you, ah, have a very explosive side to you.'

Coco's brow furrowed, and her fast breathing started up again.

'And,' Sister Veronica went on, 'I was just thinking that maybe instead of doing all the screaming and shouting all the time, and blaming your father for how miserable you seem to feel, perhaps you could use all that intense dramatic feeling to plough into your art. Really give it a good go, see what you're capable of. Like I said, you are exceptionally talented and I do believe you could produce some masterpieces.'

Coco stared at her. Then she opened her mouth.

'You're just as bad as the rest of them,' she screamed, the

sharp petulant tone that was so grating coming back with full force. 'Why are you being so horrible to me?'

'What?' Sister Veronica said, genuine surprise flooding her brain. She'd intended to be encouraging, thought she had been, had tried to give the girl's self-esteem a boost by pointing out her talent. 'What are you talking about? I haven't been horrible.'

'Yes you HAVE,' Coco shrieked. 'The tone of your voice was all hard and mean, and the expression on your face while you were talking hurt my feelings.' The girl's eyes were wide and wild, she looked like a different creature to the one she'd seen chatting into her phone the other day.

'Oh?' Sister Veronica's brain felt scrambled by these accusations. 'Well, I'm very sorry, if that's how I came across. I know I can sometimes sound gruff, but I assure you, I only intended kindness towards you. And my face? Well, I can't help that, I'm afraid. Looks the same as it always does, I fear. Perhaps I just have a serious expression on it all the time?'

'I hate all of you.' Coco picked up a heavy black stapler from the desk in front of her father. 'None of you care about me, you are all so nasty to me all the time. I never do anything to deserve it. Just leave me alone.' She hurled the stapler hard and it hit the tightly-stacked shelves next to the desk. A flurry of loose paper and a waterfall of books fell from the shelves, tumbling all over the place, and scattering themselves across the study floor like giant rectangular snowflakes. Coco turned and stormed out of the room, trying to slam the door, but finding her brother had arrived to witness the proceedings and was currently propping it open.

'Don't worry about her,' Wilfred said, a cheeriness to his voice as Coco's loud footsteps disappeared down the corridor. 'She's as mentally unbalanced as Romilly. It must be genetic. I've found the best way to deal with her is just to ignore it all. She's only happy when she's trying to impress her idiot followers on Instagram.'

Sister Veronica stared at Florence, feeling genuinely flabber-gasted. She'd thought some sensible talking would help the girl, but Coco hadn't responded in the way she'd hoped at all. She'd never come across such an illogical reaction to words that were meant to be bolstering before. Magnus let out a big sigh.

'I'm sorry, Sister,' he said, shaking his head. 'Don't take it personally, she's like that with everyone. She's always in trouble at school for being rude to the teachers, and for flouncing out of lessons. I think it's become her way of getting attention, you know, any attention is good, sort of thing. I know some of it's my fault, I haven't been very emotionally accessible for the children, I think I've been depressed for a long time, and I know I've handled that badly. But I'm trying to change that now and make different choices. Although it seems that for Coco, there might be a long road ahead.'

'Maybe we need to call in some professional help?' Florence said. 'You know, get her assessed or something?'

'Perhaps,' Magnus said, the look of habitual defeat shadowing his face once more. 'It's just so hard to know what to do.'

'Dad,' Wilfred said. 'Do you want to come and see my 3D nativity scene? I've made it using dinosaurs instead of people.'

'That sounds great, Wilfred.' Magnus turned towards his son. 'But I think I should tidy up this mess in here first.'

'No,' Florence said, a firmness to her voice. 'You go with Wilfred, Magnus. It will do you good to spend some time together. I'll sort the study out. And I'm sure V won't mind helping.'

Sister Veronica nodded.

'Okay, thank you, both of you.' Magnus, looking brighter, stood up and followed his son – who was looking very pleased – from the room.

'Honestly, that girl,' Florence said, going over to a jumble of books on the floor. 'There's something in her tone, when she gets going, that makes me want to run for the hills. It gets under my skin, do you know what I mean? It's like someone running their fingernails down an old-fashioned blackboard; just unbearable.'

Sister Veronica suppressed a smile.

'Yes,' she said. 'I do. I honestly thought I was being positive, trying to get her to feel good about her art.' She bent down and started to pick up various loose sheets of paper, and a variety of envelopes and other odds and ends.

'Oh, don't pay any attention to Coco,' Florence said. 'I've tried all sorts of different approaches with her, but nothing seems to work. She's a bloody nightmare, just like her mother. Wilfred was right about that. My only hope is that Coco will grow out of it eventually, now that she's not living with Romilly.'

They worked diligently, clearing up the mess, stacking piles of paper back on the shelves, and tidily arranging the books. Neat footsteps got louder in the corridor outside the room and Mrs Hardman's head appeared at the door.

'Mrs Beresford?' she said. 'Lunch is ready.'

'Oh, thank you, Mrs Hardman,' Florence said, straightening up. She looked around. 'V, do you mind finishing in here if I go and round everyone up? It always takes at least ten minutes for them all to arrive at the table after they've been told, for some reason. I always feel like I'm trying to herd cats with this family.'

Sister Veronica smiled at her cousin.

'Yes, you go,' she said. 'We're nearly done in here, there's just that mess under the chair to go now.'

As Florence exited the room, following Mrs Hardman down the corridor, Sister Veronica slowly dropped to her knees and scooped out the papers from under the swivel chair, attempting to stack them into a neat pile. One in particular caught her attention. It wasn't a loose sheet like the rest of them; someone had taken the time to fold whatever it was into the tiniest shape possible, as though trying to hide whatever was written on it. Curiosity got the better of her, and – berating herself for being so dashed nosy – she unfolded the paper and read its contents. Then she reread them again, just to make sure she'd got it right the first time, feeling her heart speed up inside her chest. Could the information here be true? Surely not. But then again, if it was, it made sense out of several things that had been troubling her over the last few days.

Her hands trembling, Sister Veronica quickly refolded the paper and stuffed it into the deep pocket of her skirt. All the Saints in Heaven, that had been a shock. She now had a very good idea about who it had been that murdered Giles, and possibly Digby too.

36

Everyone was already seated for once, Sister Veronica observed, as she entered the dining room, trying to create a normal expression on her face but with chills spreading out under her skin. The room abounded with delicious aromas of apple, fennel and chestnut, coming from Mrs Hardman's carefully prepared lunch. The steaming plates were already on the table, and she sat down at the one plate left, Florence to her left, Magnus to her right, and Wilfred opposite her. Coco, she noticed, obviously having had one of her mercurial quick mood changes, was chatting happily away to Araminta – who was drinking water, a much more subdued expression on her face than usual. Rufus was absent, he must still be out, brooding over Araminta's decision to be honest about their desperate scheme, she thought. Maud and Barnaby sat together, both surveying the goings-on before them, munching steadily. Cecily, seated very far away from her husband – Sister Veronica couldn't help but wonder whose decision that was – was for once looking her age if not older. She was wearing sunglasses, her skin sallow, and she toyed with a piece of meat listlessly. *Hungover*, Sister Veronica thought. *Serves her right. I hope she's regretting her awful outburst yesterday, she should be ashamed of herself.* A large red patch covered half of Cecily's face, probably from where Florence's scalding hot chocolate had landed. *That looks painful,* she thought. *It's a real shame her reckless actions had to come to physical injury. Things could have been handled so differently.* Ophelia and Sam sat together, chatting quietly, both seeming much more relaxed than ever before. Lucie's appearance surprised her the most. The girl seemed defeated somehow, as though she had the weight of the world on her shoulders. Her face was different, drawn. What on earth could have happened to cause that?

The murderer, she knew, was present at the table. And she hoped to goodness she was acting as she normally would, despite the icy fear she felt at being in their presence. It was important she carried on as usual for now, she didn't want to alert them to her new knowledge just yet, didn't want to trigger them into any hasty, reckless actions, or to give them an opportunity to escape from justice. After lunch, she would explain what she knew to Florence privately, and the two of them would quietly call the police, ask them to come to the house and arrest the perpetrator, show them the evidence. Until then, she would have to go along with it all and try not to let on that she now knew the truth.

Magnus tapped the side of his glass – the noise making Sister Veronica jump – as Mrs Hardman came in, with a big jug of water. They all had soft drinks today, Sister Veronica noticed. For once.

'I'd like to make a toast before we all get too stuck in,' he said. 'To Mrs Hardman, for the exceptional meals she continues to make us.'

Muted cheers of 'hear hear', and 'absolutely top notch' came from up and down the table. Sister Veronica tried not to look at the killer, didn't want to give herself away, but it was hard. Her eyes kept naturally going in that direction. Mrs Hardman gave a small smile, bowed her head, and retreated from the room.

'And,' Magnus said, 'I would like to thank my mother, Florence, for inviting so many of us to Chalfield Hall this year.' He turned to her. 'I know it's been pretty shocking here recently, for so many unforeseen reasons, and you've had to cope with so much. I know you're probably trying to grieve for Dad with all of us milling around and getting in the way, yet you are still going out of your way to make us feel welcome, and I want to say thank you for that. I'm glad you've had Sister Veronica here as a support for you.' He turned and smiled at her, then took a deep breath. 'As well as being appalling, events here have also triggered off a turning point, for me at least,' he said, his voice beginning to choke up. 'I'm sorry, Mum, for not coping and for letting you down over the past few years. But I'm really going to try to get life back on track now.' He sat down, wiping his eyes, this time to a more elevated chorus of support. Florence reached over and patted his hand.

'Thank you for saying that,' she said, giving her son a warm smile.

'Right, let's dig in properly,' Barnaby said, staring down at what was left of his food. 'I'm afraid I can't wait another moment.'

Conversation dropped as the feast disappeared from the plates. Mrs Hardman really did have a knack with flavours, Sister Veronica noticed – despite her near critical levels of anxiety – as a taste explosion occurred in her mouth. She'd lived through many tragedies in her life, but had never yet found anything that had put her off food. *I'll need the energy later*, she decided, making good headway into the pile before her. *This lot should keep me going for a while.* Still, she wasn't enjoying her Christmas Eve lunch, the evil near her was too potent for that.

The food was much needed fuel, as far as she was concerned, and the fact that it was tasty: so much the better.

Florence coughed, putting down her knife and fork.

'Are you okay, Flo?' Sister Veronica turned to her cousin.

'I think I've got something stuck in my throat.' Florence grasped at her neck. 'I can't breathe, V. It feels like something is swelling down there. Help me, please.'

With a feeling of alarm washing through her, Sister Veronica put down her cutlery, reaching over to pat Florence on the back.

'There,' she said. 'Is that any better?'

'No,' Florence said, her voice sounding strangled. 'It's getting worse.'

37

Most of the party had stopped talking, and were now watching Sister Veronica rise quickly to her feet.

'Have a drink of water, Mum,' Magnus said, topping up her glass. But Florence wasn't listening. She was slumping sideways, her eyes rolling back in her head, a thin dribble of white froth coming out of her mouth.

'Someone help me,' Sister Veronica shouted, and in seconds Lucie and Magnus were helping her half carry, half drag Florence onto the floor. She was making a strange growling sound.

'Her lips are turning blue,' Lucie said. She turned round. 'For God's sake, can one of you useless lumps call Auntie Florence an ambulance instead of just sitting there staring?'

'I will,' Wilfred said, retrieving his phone from his pocket, and punching in the numbers.

Sister Veronica, white, cold fear taking over her body and mind, started slapping her cousin's back.

'Try to be sick, Flo,' she said loudly. 'I think you've been poisoned. Try and throw the whole lot up.'

'Poisoned?' Magnus turned to her. 'She can't have been. If Mum had, surely the whole lot of us would be ill too?'

'I'll explain later,' Sister Veronica said, thumping away. 'Call the police as well, Wilfred.' *I'm not going to lose Flo*, she thought wildly. *Not now, not after we've all been through so much. Come on, God, Universe, or whoever you are. Help me out here, please. Flo deserves to live. She has to survive, to thrive after this awful Christmas is over. Please, give her another chance at life.*

Florence was now writhing on the carpet in a desperate, jerky way. Her convulsions became bigger, and it seemed as though she was straining from her stomach. Then in one painful movement, she vomited the contents of her lunch onto the carpet. Her body became still. Sister Veronica, kneeling next to her cousin, stroked her clammy forehead, watching her face intently for signs of change. Florence was no longer struggling, and her distressed expression was relaxing. After a moment or two her eyes came back into focus. She stared upwards.

'Ah, you're back with us,' Sister Veronica said, relief washing out much of the intense anxiety in her. 'How are you feeling, Flo?'

'Bloody awful,' Florence said, closing her eyes. 'I think I must have eaten something bad. Just give me a minute and I'll be okay.'

'Now, you lie still, Flo,' Sister Veronica said. 'The ambulance is on its way.' *She can't remember anything I said about poison*, she thought. *She must have gone unconscious for a few seconds.*

'Ambulance?' Florence's eyes opened again. 'I don't need one of those, I'll be up and about soon. Just let me lie here for a bit.'

'Well, they'll be here soon,' Wilfred called from his place at the table. 'So will the police.'

'Police?' Florence said, angst in her voice. 'Why on earth are they coming?'

'I'm not sure, Mum,' Magnus said, bringing a drink over to her. He looked at Sister Veronica, his eyebrows raised.

'Don't you worry about a thing for now, Flo,' Sister Veronica said. 'Just concentrate on feeling better.'

Now that the point of danger had clearly passed, she heaved herself back up onto her feet. All the original party were still present, except one person. Maud. *Dash it all, she must have slipped out when Florence was at her worst*, she thought. *I don't know what to do; do I stay with Flo and make sure she's all right, or go and find Maud?* She looked around. Cecily was still slumped at the table wearing her sunglasses. Barnaby was watching the proceedings, a much more engaged look on his face than usual. Coco was quiet for once. Perhaps seeing a real-life drama unfold in front of her had been a shock, made her lose the impetus for starting her own spectacle? She doubted the impact would last for long. Magnus was fussing over his mother, making sure she drank some water. It was nice, in a way, to see him taking care of Florence for once, Sister Veronica thought, instead of the other way around. Lucie – ever the practical one – still looking defeated, with a grim expression on her face, was carrying in an armful of blankets and cushions, and set about making her aunt as comfortable as possible. Araminta got up to help her. Wilfred, now tucking into his lunch with gusto, moved his chair a little so Ophelia and Sam could squeeze past.

'I think I'll take Sam out into the garden for a bit,' Ophelia said. 'Seeing Florence collapse has set him back a bit, and I want him to leave trauma behind from now on, in as much as that's possible. Hopefully he'll learn to trust that the world isn't just a scary place to be one day.'

Sister Veronica nodded. She saw Sam's fearful, pale face looking up at her, and smiled warmly at him. The poor boy.

'Quite right,' she said. 'Go and have some fun together. You both deserve it.' *Until the police come back and want to talk to you,* she added in her mind. *But then, we'll all explain how we witnessed Digby's abuse, and hopefully they will be lenient.*

'Magnus?' she said, turning towards him. 'I just have to go and check on something important for a minute. I can see you're looking after your mother very well, I'll leave her in your capable hands for a little while.'

'Yeah, yeah that's fine,' he said, distracted, not really listening.

Sister Veronica exited the dining room and walked down the corridor, her heartbeats ratcheting up to a continuous fast drumming. Where would she find Maud? Was it wise to approach the woman before the police got there? Probably not, a tiny part of her answered. But she was going to do it anyway, because she was too bloody-minded for her own good. *And I'm angry now*, she thought, feeling the folded-up paper in her skirt. She no longer felt fear; her drumming heart was down to adrenaline. The heat rising in her was caused by a furious realisation that she should have worked all this out much earlier on, so that poor Flo didn't have to suffer like she just had. *What gives anyone the right to take away someone's life for their own gain?* she thought as she thumped along. *Even if there is a type of sick, twisted love behind it all. Let me find you, Maud, and ask you that question to your face. Then we'll see what you have to say for yourself.*

38

Rufus drained the bitter dregs of his pint of Dragons Best, and slapped the glass back down on the table. The oh-so familiar feeling of intoxication was washing through him, and it had never been more welcome, never so urgently needed to obliterate his intense emotions.

'Same again?' Steven, Romilly's brother said, his vowels and consonants all slurring together.

'I'll have a double gin and tonic this time,' Romilly said, almost falling off her bar stool in her eagerness to put her order in. She was looking more dishevelled than usual; there were strands coming loose from her ponytail and there was a big mascara smudge under one of her eyes.

Rufus nodded. It was a bit of luck, he reflected, that he'd run into Romilly and her brother in Little Ashby's only pub, The Grey Horse. He'd hotfooted it straight down there after his argument with Minty; desperate for sustenance and the elimination of unmanageable feelings. It was a small, cosy place, with an open fire burning in the grate. Romilly and her brother had already been stuck in when he'd arrived – dizzy with fury at his wife's stupidity – with empty glasses and crisp packets scattered all over their table. Of course, they'd invited him to join them, cleared their coats from the spare chair, and motioned for him to sit down.

What good would come from being honest with the family about the notes they'd been leaving? Rufus thought for the fiftieth time that day as he watched Steven stagger over to the bar. For God's sake, Minty was ridiculous if she actually thought Florence would roll over and forgive them for what they'd done. They'd be cut out of any inheritance for ever now, and they bloody deserved to get some more than most people in that godforsaken house, considering how badly Giles had treated them. Rufus had lost nearly half a million, his entire pension plan because of that stupid man. And now Araminta has an attack of conscience and plans to reveal all? It was the most foolish, crazy, irrational thing she'd ever said. After Araminta and alcohol, the one thing Rufus loved best was money. And at least two of those three were evading him at the moment, so, true to habit, he was drowning his misery in the third. And right now it felt brilliant.

'Giles was a bastard,' Romilly was saying to him. 'Through and through. He treated us all badly, and Florence should right his wrongs.' It was funny to see her so drunk, Rufus thought. It took a lot to get him even slightly tipsy nowadays, as he drank so frequently his alcohol tolerance was very high, but the double shots he'd consumed shortly after entering The Grey Horse had got him off to a good start. He *did* enjoy watching other people get squiffy though, never tired of the amusement, of belly-laughing at them as they embarrassed themselves. It was great sport. And interestingly, right now Romilly was letting her usual barriers down, becoming more honest and lucid than ever before about Giles.

'You should drink more often, Rom, it suits you.' He winked at her.

'I drink with Steven now, most evenings,' she said. 'He's turned to whisky as a comfort ever since Giles fired him. He's never been able to get another job, I think his self-esteem is too damaged now. All because of that thieving bastard.'

They'd already all established, shortly after Rufus' arrival, that the three of them had found out in various ways about Giles embezzling money from his failing business. Steven confided that he'd been fired after threatening to expose Giles to the rest of the factory's workforce, but Giles – being in Rufus' opinion the arrogant heartless sod he was – had said if Steven did so he'd cut Coco and Wilfred out of his will entirely, and that Steven would have only himself to blame for their demise. Knowing Giles still had Chalfield Hall under his belt to leave to the family after he'd gone, Steven had explained to Rufus that he'd had no other choice but to capitulate to Giles' demands in order to save his niece and nephew's chance of inheritance. Rufus reckoned, by the look of the man, that the bile and resentment of the whole situation had chewed away at him ever since. He was a wreck, skinny, hollow-faced and miserable, without a good word to say for anyone. Not the kind of man Rufus usually liked to associate with, but an adequate drinking partner for the day. Besides, he thought, watching Steven wobble back over with a full tray of drinks, a plan of retribution was now forming in his mind, and Steven and Romilly would be necessary appendages to its success, if he won them over favourably enough. A new round of drinks was a good place to start.

'Cheers everyone,' he said, grasping the full glass Steven was holding out to him. 'Let's drink to Christmas Eve, and to all the Scrooges of the world.'

39

Sister Veronica waited outside Maud's bedroom door, listening for any sound from inside. The smell of the woman's flowery perfume hung in the air. Nothing. She pushed the door with her foot and it swung open. The room was empty, except for a blue suitcase lying in the middle of the bed. *So Maud must still be around in Chalfield Hall somewhere. She would have had time to return to her room and grab her suitcase, what with all the kerfuffle with Florence, if she'd been intending to leave the house for good.*

Padding off as quietly as she could, which wasn't very due to the old house's creaking floorboards, Sister Veronica searched the upstairs, then took herself back down the sweeping staircase and looked in the living room, conservatory, study, and kitchen. Of course, there was the old back living room, now never used, that had been mad old Henrietta's favourite place to sit and hold court in, she remembered. An eerie feeling came over her as she found it and opened the door, remembering how she'd hated going into that dark room as a child. Not much had changed in there, it was a place frozen in time. White covers had been thrown over the furniture and collections of cobwebs and dust abounded in all the corners; the musty smell of past memories pervading throughout. She remembered how mad old Henrietta, always dressed in black, would grab any child who had displeased her, and keep them in a tight hold on her lap for hours as a punishment. It hadn't happened to her much, she'd always liked to please the adults and rarely stepped out of line. But Tarquin had been a cheeky boy, and she could see him now – squirming and calling out as Henrietta held him tightly on her knee in the dark room for what seemed like eons – a sentence for a mild misdemeanour.

The room was empty – no Maud. Feeling grateful that she did not have to enter the space, but increasingly confused about where on earth the woman could be, Sister Veronica closed the door and walked on. She checked the various storage rooms, the utility area, all the large walk-in cupboards and the pantry. She even forced herself to go down into the wine cellar, and look around the cold, dark place, taking a brief walk among the racks of bottles. *No one there, thank the Saints.*

Now for the garden, she thought, puffing back up the stairs into the much more welcome bright kitchen. The rooms that Giles and Florence had recently done up were much lighter and more inviting than the rest of the house, she thought, walking out into the biting winter air. Perhaps that was Florence's reasoning behind the renovations; an attempt to bring the house out of the dark ages and make it a friendlier, warmer environment. The large front living room was cosy, too, but the rest of the house was still chilly and Gothic, so dimly lit, with a plethora of cold décor and furniture. It didn't help that most of the windows were so small – the lack of light added to its peculiar atmosphere. For a moment she wondered if mad old Henrietta lived on there as a ghost, haunting her favourite room, and gliding down the rest of the corridors at night, hoping to scare the wits out of an unsuspecting family member. Then she reprimanded herself for being so ridiculous and said a prayer to the universe, apologising in case she'd offended anyone out there with her thoughts of the dead, God rest their souls.

Heading through the herb garden and wrapping her arms round herself to ward off the cold, Sister Veronica thought about Maud's connection to the family. She didn't actually know much about the woman, just that she was Giles' only surviving cousin, and that she'd always seemed like a harmless part of the furniture – turning up at family gatherings when they were all young – just after Flo had met her future husband and Sister Veronica was a novice nun – and smiling vacantly at everyone but never giving away much of her personality. She must have enjoyed the gatherings then, always turned up but seemed happy on the outside. Maud's past was a mystery to her, she hardly knew anything about it, and felt slightly ashamed that she'd never asked. As far as she knew the woman had never married. And up until a couple of hours ago, she'd been pretty sure that she'd never had any children.

She checked in and around the summer house but there was no sign of life. Trudging over the frosty grass, she headed towards the moss-stained greenhouse. Ah, was that a movement she saw through the uncleaned windows? Yes, there was another one. As she got closer, she saw that it was indeed Maud in there. The woman appeared to be standing by the door. She turned the handle and opened it as Sister Veronica approached.

'Hello, Sister,' Maud said, giving a neat smile. She took a step to one side. 'I've been waiting for you. Do come in.'

40

Now even Rufus was feeling hammered. He knew he was, because he was starting to believe he was the most important, charming, friendly person in the whole pub, and was acting accordingly. This, he knew from past experience, was a sign that he might be getting slightly out of control. It was as though he was observing himself from the outside in; listening to himself gabble on at Romilly and Steven, watching his huge hand gestures as he explained his foolproof plan of reparation to them, unable to stop himself from acting like an inebriated idiot, or more accurately – a fool.

'None of us ever deserved to be treated so shoddily by Giles,' he was saying to them, his eyes intent. 'Can't you see? The man was a tyrant, he robbed me of my savings, and you, Steven, of months of wages, and more importantly, your job. All so he could keep up his deluded fantasy of being a successful, rich businessman. It's madness, the reality must be known. We need to be the ones to tell everyone what Giles was really up to. And we have to do it right now, go to Chalfield Hall and take charge of the situation. Tell everyone what we know, and force Florence to put it right. Are you with me?'

'Yes,' Steven said. He tried to put his glass back down on the table but missed. Romilly gasped as she watched the remaining drink land inside her open handbag.

'Sorry, Rom,' Steven said, barely able to open his eyes. 'I'll buy you a new one.'

'You don't have enough money to buy me a new bag,' Romilly said, her words slurring.

'Which is exactly why we need to go and confront Florence,' Rufus said, standing up, using the tabletop as leverage. 'Come on, chaps, now's the time. Let's go and take back what is ours.'

'Fine with me.' Steven staggered to his feet, bumping into the table.

'Oh, all right then.' Romilly tried to stand up, too, but couldn't. The men each took hold of one of her arms and lifted her upright, which took quite an effort due to her enormous height and weight. In a strange, three-legged race kind of effort, they made their way slowly out of the pub in a huddle.

'To Chalfield Hall!' Rufus punched the air once they were outside, as snowflakes began to fall all around them. 'The revolution has begun.' Unsteady on their feet, and swaying slightly, they set off in the direction of the house.

41

Sister Veronica, inwardly berating herself for taking such a risk, stepped inside the greenhouse. Maud shut the door behind her and stood against it, blocking any possibility of an escape.

'So you've been waiting for me?' Sister Veronica said, looking the woman straight in the eyes. 'Why would that be then?' An earthy smell filled the air around them.

'Because you're a nosy old crow who can't keep out of other people's business.' Maud smiled gently in her usual way, but her eyes were hard, cold. Sister Veronica felt the adrenaline pump round her insides with even greater haste.

'Well that's as maybe,' Sister Veronica said, feeling in her skirt pocket for the folded paper. She grasped it, pulled it out and unfolded it. 'But I can tell you one thing, Maud. My inquisitive nature often leads me to uncover truths that other people try to hide.'

Maud stared at the yellowing document. Sister Veronica turned it round so they could both see the typed writing on it. The letters were slightly uneven and it looked as though an old-fashioned typewriter had been used to produce the legal statement.

'It says here that you are Ophelia's birth mother,' she said quietly. 'Doesn't it, Maud?'

The woman hadn't taken her eyes from the paper. A long minute passed without either of them saying anything.

'So what if I am?' Maud said eventually.

'Is that why you've been doing all this?' Sister Veronica risked a quick look out of the grimy window, rather hoping to spot another human being in the garden. Preferably the police. But there was no one, just some gently swirling snowflakes, some now settling on the ground. 'For Ophelia?'

'Doing what?' Maud turned to her. 'I'm not quite sure what you're talking about, Sister.' A slightly confused expression washed over her plump face but her eyes remained as focused as a hawk's.

Sister Veronica sighed.

'Look, I know it was you who killed Giles,' she said. 'And Digby. And at lunch you tried to murder Florence too, didn't you, Maud?'

Maud stared at her.

'Did I?' she said. 'Have you got any evidence to prove your wild claims, Sister?'

'I have a motive for you.' Sister Veronica glanced at the paper she held. 'A very persuasive one, in fact. It clearly states here, that you are Ophelia's birth mother, and that you willingly gave her up for adoption to Tarquin and Marina all those years ago. What happened, Maud? That must have been a very stressful time for you. What on earth went on that led to you having to give your own flesh and blood away?' Sister Veronica, swallowing down the anger she felt for the attack on Florence, was trying to breathe calmly. She wanted answers, wanted Maud to explain herself before anything else happened. The police would be arriving any minute if Wilfred made the call correctly and then she could hand the whole mess over to them. Until then, she would try and get as much information out of the woman as possible, and the best way to do that, she thought, was to seem as calm and understanding as she could.

'Stressful?' Maud repeated. 'Oh yes, Sister, it was just a tiny bit taxing, being forced to give away my beloved daughter.'

Ah, Sister Veronica thought, nodding. *Now we might be getting somewhere.*

'I'm so sorry, Maud,' she said. 'For everything you've had to go through. Who made you give Ophelia up for adoption?'

'My parents,' Maud said, and for once her nondescript smile had been replaced by a look of hatred. 'I'd become close to my father's apprentice, David Gilbey. He lived with us for a while, so him and Father could get up early to work in the bakery. We weren't as rich as Giles back then, Sister. Giles' fortune is all new money, self-made. His parents and mine came from much more lowly stock, you know. I was in love with David, at least for a time. When I found out I was expecting a child I was terrified, back then being an unmarried mother brought shame on the whole family, and I knew my parents would be horrified when they found out. They'd always been hard on me, they weren't naturally very parental. They believed that the more severe they were, the better I'd turn out.'

'So you tried to hide your growing belly,' Sister Veronica said. 'I can totally understand, Maud. You must have been so fearful of their reaction.'

'I was.' Maud nodded slightly. 'I was hoping David would make an honest woman of me, ask me to marry him. But he never did, underneath it all he was a coward. Once he found out I was pregnant he handed his resignation to my father and moved away.'

Sister Veronica shook her head.

'I'm very sorry to hear that,' she said, meaning it. A few men – and sometimes women – were indeed cowards when it came to parenthood, for some reason shirking responsibility, unable to look after the perfect little human they'd created, unwilling to support the woman they'd so readily impregnated.

'Obviously I grew so big that my mother noticed one day,' Maud said, tears glistening at the corners of her eyes. 'She told my father and they shouted at me, called me a cheap whore. My mother said I would stay inside the house until the baby was born, then I would give it up for adoption immediately. One day, my mother's father – Henrietta's brother Hugh – told her that Henrietta's son Tarquin and his wife Marina had found they couldn't have children, and were desperate to adopt a child. "Perfect," my mother said. "We can keep it all in the family, no one ever need know." She negotiated the adoption with Tarquin and Marina, her only terms were that no one ever be told who Ophelia's parents were, not even anyone in the family. There just needed to be one document, she'd found out, to make the whole thing legal, but other than that the baby's parentage could remain a secret. Tarquin and Marina readily agreed, and kept their word. They never told anyone. The only proof that I'm Ophelia's mother is on the paper you have in your hand. Goodness knows how it came to be in Giles' study, but I suppose Henrietta's affairs passed on to him and Florence when she died. If he ever read the paper and knew about it, he never told me.'

'No,' Sister Veronica said. 'I don't think Florence knows either. Everyone certainly did a good job of keeping the whole matter hidden. But why go to all this trouble to erase Giles? What on earth was the point of that, Maud?' Her brow crinkled as she tried to understand.

'I suppose I can tell you more about it now, Sister,' Maud said. 'The truth is that I'm dying.'

Sister Veronica renewed her stare into the woman's eyes.

'Is that why the hospital called the other day?' she said.

'Yes.' Maud nodded. 'I have end-stage lymphoma that's spread throughout my body. Tumours everywhere, not that you would know it to look at me. I wear a lot of rouge on my cheeks to look as healthy as possible, and although I have lost quite a lot of weight I'm still big, so people don't suspect there's anything wrong with me. There's nothing more the doctors can do now, I've been through all the treatments over the last two years and they haven't worked. But I knew there was a gift I could give my daughter before I died, and I was hoping to do it without any nosy old busybody interfering.' She glared.

'Go on,' Sister Veronica said.

'Giles ran a very successful business,' Maud said. *Ah*, Sister Veronica thought. *She obviously doesn't know about Beresford's Breaded Wonders failing, and about Giles siphoning off what was left of the money.* 'And he and Florence own Chalfield Hall. I saw his will one day – I know Florence will have made out a separate one and I've never seen that, only Giles' – and I saw that after Florence, the next person he would leave his estate to is me, being his only living blood relative. And obviously the person I would leave all my assets to is my daughter, Ophelia.'

'Oh I *see*,' Sister Veronica said, understanding Maud's skewed logic all at once. 'So you thought that by killing off Giles and Florence, you would inherit everything from the business and maybe something from the house and then leave it all to Ophelia? And you got up earlier than usual and left me that poison pen letter, warning me to stop interfering – by which you meant helping Florence get to the bottom of who was behind her husband's demise – because you wanted your plan to be carried out without interruptions?'

Maud nodded.

'She was taken away from me the day after her birth, Sister.' A tear ran down Maud's cheek. 'As soon as I saw her I felt a love so powerful that I can't describe it. She was as beautiful then as she is now. I haven't been able to give her much, but I wanted to make sure she would be looked after long after I was gone. And to do that I needed to give her money.'

'And you never thought that maybe Florence might have left a separate will, passing on everything to Magnus, if anything was to happen to her, after Giles' death?' Sister Veronica said, her voice gentle. 'I don't think it works as simply as that, Maud. The house would never have gone to you, it gets passed down in Florence's family, and would go to whoever Florence stated in her will.'

'But Beresford's Breaded Wonders is different,' Maud said. 'I've seen Giles' will, I know he left it to me, after Florence. And that's *his* property, nothing to do with your side of the family at all.'

'That's true.' Sister Veronica nodded, trying to level out her breathing. There was no way she was going to enlighten the woman about the fact that there was nothing left in Giles' business at all at this stage, other than a hefty debt. She could see Maud was getting angry and didn't want to inflame the situation more than she needed to.

'And Digby?' she said. 'What about him, Maud?'

Maud's eyes raged.

'Every time I've seen Ophelia since Sam was born, she's seemed more and more miserable,' Maud said. 'I may not be a relationship expert, Sister, but I know what misery feels like, goodness knows I've felt enough in my life. I knew there was something wrong in that marriage, and I could see Digby wasn't treating her nicely, even before you lot picked up on it. The way he carried on when Lucie confronted him was the last straw. I had to free my daughter, and as the doctors have only given me a few months to live, it had to be now, this Christmas. I knew I'd never get another chance. And I don't regret doing it, she and

Sam are free to live as they choose now, happily hopefully, without that abusive bastard of a man breathing down their necks.'

Sister Veronica nodded. This decision of Maud's was easier for her to understand. Although totally criminal and heinous, Maud's act of freeing Ophelia from Digby's terrorising was almost fathomable, especially as she felt she had nothing to lose.

'I don't suppose you understand me, Sister,' Maud said. 'You've never had any children, you've never felt the all-consuming love that comes over a parent, where you would do anything – literally anything at all – to make sure your child is looked after and happy.'

'No,' Sister Veronica said. 'But my life has not been without tragedy, Maud. It seems you and I never really got to know each other, and if that's my doing then I'm very sorry.'

'I'm sorry too, Sister,' Maud said, her hand going to a shelf and retrieving a long strand of thick garden wire. 'Especially because of what has to happen now. You are not so bad, I can see that now. Interfering, but with a good heart. I am truly sorry for what I'm about to do.'

'And what's that?' Sister Veronica said, her eyes on the wire.

'Kill you,' Maud said, her fat hands grasping the wire at each end and bringing it up towards Sister Veronica's throat. 'Can't you see that you know too much now?'

42

'Florence,' Rufus shouted through the letter box. 'I know you're in there. Have some God-damn courage and come and open the door this instant.'

Florence, now lying on one of the sofas in the living room, closed her eyes.

'I'm so sorry about him.' Araminta stroked her aunt's hair. 'He doesn't usually get this bad when he's drunk, he must have had loads. Just ignore him and he'll have to go away and sleep it off somewhere. I'm furious with him, Auntie Florence. Right at this moment I could murder the man.'

'Don't talk like that, dear,' Florence said, her voice weak. 'I think we've had enough deaths round here for one Christmas, don't you?'

Lucie's voice floated over to them. She was in the corner, talking to Neil on the phone.

'No, I can't come back at the moment,' she was saying. 'Yes I know I said I was coming back today but something awful happened to Auntie Florence, she collapsed, I thought she was going to die, Neil. I have to stay here, just for a bit longer, until I know she's all right.'

The busy sound of a group of vehicles trundling down the drive with their sirens blaring filled the living room, and in seconds blue flashing lights were shining through the windows and bouncing off the mirror on the wall.

'Ah, the paramedics and police are here at last,' Wilfred said, sounding happy. 'They took their time. There must have been another emergency in Northampton or something.' He went off to open the front door. 'Hey,' Florence heard him shout. 'Don't push past me like that, Rufus, you just hurt my arm.'

Florence turned her head to find a bedraggled bunch of three grouping before her; Rufus, Steven and Romilly. The sour stench of alcohol exuding from them was too much, it made her stomach lurch again, and she turned her head away. Why was this Christmas so hellish? And to think, she'd invited her cousin Veronica here to try and get to the bottom of the poison pen letters, only to have her unwittingly plunged into the murky events of the last few days. Giles' murder and the sickening sight of Digby dead on the hall floor almost made the horror of the letters diminish to ridiculousness. Almost, but not quite. And here Rufus was, out of his mind again on alcohol, standing shouting at her in the soft glow of the Christmas tree lights. It was all too much, she didn't think she could take any more. She was going to find V and make a plan for them both to leave the house as soon as possible, try and find an immediate cottage to rent somewhere. She so desperately wanted to get away from everything, it was a physical feeling in her blood, willing her – urging her – to travel far away from it all.

'Go away,' Araminta shouted at her husband and the other two. 'How *dare* you just barge in here when my aunt's feeling so unwell. You should be ashamed of yourselves. Get out this instant. Officer?' she called to the uniformed man who had just entered the room. 'Please escort my husband off the premises. He's causing an unwanted scene.'

'I haven't even *started* causing an unwanted scene, actually, Minty,' Rufus shouted back, his voice thick and rough. 'I've come to talk to Florence – and everyone else – about her bastard husband, that crook Giles. Florence is involved in his dirty plans up to her neck, too, I'd bet my last pound on it. No, I'm not going away, Minty. Steven and Romilly and I are going to stay here until we get some answers.'

'What's going on here now?' Florence heard DI Ahuja's voice cut through the commotion. She tried to sit up, but immediately felt dizzy and leaned back again.

'Lucie?' she said, as she saw her niece ring off. 'Where's V? I need her here now. Please find her.'

'I don't know where she is.' Lucie walked towards her. 'I had a quick look before but she seems to have disappeared. The last time I saw her was just after you collapsed. She went off saying she was going to make a quick check on something, but never came back. Maud's vanished too.'

'Oh no.' Florence shook her head, her face pale. 'I've got a bad feeling about this. Veronica's not the vanishing type. Something must have happened. Quick, let's all go and look for her.'

'Nobody,' Rufus shouted, his voice uncontrolled, 'is going anywhere, until Florence gives me all my money back.'

It was in the silent few seconds that followed his outburst that Sister Veronica's faint, desperate, guttural shouts for help could be heard.

43

For someone who'd only been given a few months to live, Maud turned out to be surprisingly strong and persistent. It was all Sister Veronica could do to keep kicking her away. Now on the floor, with her feet peddling the woman away from her, she could feel a wetness running down her neck from where Maud had initially nicked her with the wire. She stared up into the woman's face. Now that she could see her at close quarters, Maud did look ill. Sickly in fact; her skin was grey under the rouge, and she had dark blue bags under her eyes. Her hair was thinning, perhaps from some treatment or other, and there were sparse patches in places on her scalp that she must have kept disguised with her hairstyle. Why hadn't she noticed all this before?

'Help!' Sister Veronica shouted again, her throat now sore from all the yelling. Where was everybody? 'Florence? Anyone? Help me! I'm in the greenhouse.'

'No one's coming.' Maud tried a new angle, stepping on Sister Veronica's short legs with both feet to keep them pressed down. Regretting her small stature, Sister Veronica struggled and tried to twist away, but in vain. 'If they could hear you they'd be here by now, wouldn't they, Sister? Now stop making this harder for yourself and just lie still.'

'Absolutely not.' Sister Veronica attempted to thrash her legs to move Maud off them, but the woman was so heavy she couldn't lift them at all. Maud, holding the thick wire taut, was now leaning towards her neck. Sister Veronica pounded at her, pushing her away with her hands, but she couldn't keep the giant weight of the woman off her for very long. She could feel her strength running out despite the adrenaline pumping through her veins. It must be all the rich food she'd eaten recently, she thought, it had sapped her energy, turned her into a lethargic lump.

'Agh,' Sister Veronica shouted, her arms giving way. Maud's hands that held the wire taut plummeted towards her neck and an icy pain sliced through her.

She heard the greenhouse door slam open and four police officers crowded into the cramped space, immediately pulling Maud away from her and removing the wire. Warm wetness oozed from her neck and when she looked down she saw her shirt was now soaked with blood.

'Maud Beresford,' one officer said, slightly out of breath as he and a colleague restrained her. 'I'm arresting you for attempted murder.' While he read Maud her rights, another officer bent down to see to Sister Veronica, her kind eyes swiftly raking over the wound on her neck.

'The paramedics are outside,' she said in a soothing voice. 'Once we've secured and neutralised the scene they'll come in and take good care of you, okay? Try not to worry, everything is going to be all right now.'

'Thank you,' Sister Veronica said, her voice weak. She knew, from the fact she could still talk, that the wound must be mostly superficial, which was a blessing – all things considered. 'Officer? You might want to take that plant over there with you for testing.' She pointed at a shrub with green leaves and bright red berries, taking care not to move her neck or head. 'I'm no expert, but I believe that may be rosary pea. It looks Christmassy but in fact has deadly properties, and if I'm correct then Maud somehow used the abrin in it to poison Giles to death. And she somehow tried to poison Florence earlier too, at lunch, but luckily Flo brought up her food before the toxic properties had a chance to take a good hold. Maud must have put something in her meal when she was helping Mrs Hardman in the kitchen.'

The officer looked at her, a surprised expression on her face.

'Thank you,' she said. 'I'll get someone to bag the plant up.' She turned round to relay the information.

'Nosy old weasel.' Maud turned and spat the words at the nun as she was being pushed out of the door, plants being knocked over on either side, her expression so different from her usual benign one. 'Just couldn't keep your nose out of my business, could you? You've ruined everything now.'

'Actually, you interfered with *my* business, Maud,' Sister Veronica said, hauling herself carefully into a sitting position, feeling more blood fall down her. She shivered, the icy blast now coming in, going right through to her bones. 'You attacked my family. You may think that what you did for Ophelia, you did out of motherly love. But it's a twisted kind of care you showed, Maud. No one should have to die for someone else's gain. You harmed my family, and you tried to kill Florence, and that is very much my business. But then you'll have time to think about all that in prison, won't you?'

'Oh, I won't be there for long.' Maud shot her a sick grin. 'I'll soon be going somewhere much more enjoyable.' The officers who were holding her arms finally managed to shove her through the door and out into the whirling snow. Sister Veronica heard one of them say, 'What's she talking about? She's not going anywhere else soon.'

'No idea,' the other replied.

As the paramedics rushed in and prepared Sister Veronica with gentle expertise for the stretcher, a deep exhaustion washed through her and she felt her eyelids closing. She could hear Florence's voice outside the greenhouse, near hysterical, asking for news of her 'dear, brave cousin', and being reassured by an officer that 'yes, the nun has been attacked but she'll live, she just has to go to hospital to be looked after.'

As the two halves of the stretcher slid underneath her, and she was picked up off the floor, with gauzes and sterile cloths adorning her neck, Sister Veronica felt herself sliding into a welcome sleep. Just before she succumbed completely to it, a beatific smile crept across her face. The awful feeling of impending doom, the warning that evil was in her midst that had tormented her since her arrival at Chalfield Hall, had finally gone. She gave way to a peace she'd craved for days, and enthusiastically fell into a deep slumber.

44

'Merry Christmas, V.' Florence's anxious face appeared next to her own. 'How are you feeling?'

Sister Veronica opened her eyes. She was lying with some grandeur on one of the living-room sofas, having been allowed to return to Chalfield Hall early on Christmas morning. Florence had been the perfect nurse since she'd arrived home, hardly leaving her side, except to bring her drinks with straws, easy-to-eat snacks, and painkillers. The large white bandage covering the best part of the front of her neck hid a long scar that had required a few stitches in places. Maud, she'd been told, had admitted everything to DI Ahuja while being questioned at Northampton police station. She'd apparently said it had been easy to poison Giles, and that she'd made him a separate pot of berry sauce using the rosary pea berries, and had put it on his plate while helping Mrs Hardman to carry in the meals that night. No one had suspected a thing at the time, she'd said, and her former secretarial job in the council's environmental hazards department had given her all the knowledge she needed about how best to go about her deed. She had tried to finish Florence off, too, but the bloody nun had made the woman be sick and had ruined everything. She was looking forward to death, apparently, and was completely unapologetic about her actions, especially about killing Digby, an act she was reportedly rather proud of, saying it had freed her daughter and grandson from the clutches of a monster. The news that Giles' business was in bankruptcy, however, had not gone down so well with Maud, by all accounts, and had resulted in her collapsing and becoming hysterical.

'Oh, fine,' Sister Veronica said, shifting round to look at her cousin, and wincing at the pain caused by doing so. 'Just a bit sore.'

Florence smiled at her, tears in her eyes as she looked from the bandage to her cousin's face.

'Thank you,' she said. 'You saved my life, V. If it hadn't been for your courage, I'm absolutely sure Maud would have finished me off for good. I can't believe I never suspected her, looking back at all the signs. Thank you so very much.'

'You don't have to keep saying that, Flo,' Sister Veronica said, giving a small smile. She reached out and patted her cousin's shoulder. 'You would have done the same for me, if the tables had been turned. I'm just glad you are okay, and that the poison didn't affect you too much yesterday. I couldn't have coped if you'd come to serious harm. Anyway, how's Ophelia doing? It must have been an awful shock for her, suddenly finding out the truth about Maud.'

'She's getting there,' Flo said, sighing. 'Poor creature, she's been through so much. And to think we all suspected her of Digby's murder, kept shooting her suspicious glances. And now she finds out Maud is not only her mother, but murdered two people, thinking it was in her long-lost daughter's best interests. Goodness gracious, this has been an unusual few days to say the least. Ophelia's still upstairs with the police psychiatrist, who's an absolute angel, by the way, working wonders with her. She'll be all right, I think, with time.'

'Well, it's only natural that we all thought the girl did it, under the circumstances,' Sister Veronica said, her voice gruff. She'd thought it had been Ophelia, too, and was questioning her own judgement about that. *The simplest answer isn't always the right one*, she thought. *Always look deeper into things, Veronica. Listen to your gut feeling.* 'Who's looking after Sam?' she said.

'Well.' Florence's expression brightened. 'You'll never believe it, but Coco has really stepped up to the mark, since the whole kerfuffle yesterday. She's really taken him under her wing, in a way she's never done with Wilfred. I think that what happened with you shocked her into growing up a bit. They are doing some art in the kitchen, Coco's teaching him about all the different colours and how they go together. She's brought loads of her art supplies down. She even told him she might go to art college one day, which is an absolute turnaround and a wonderful step forward for her. And you'll never guess what, V...'

Sister Veronica looked at her.

'Coco came to find me this morning and actually apologised for her behaviour.' Florence shook her head, smiling. 'I couldn't believe it, she's never said sorry for anything before. It actually brought tears to my eyes, and I gave her the biggest hug.'

Sister Veronica chuckled.

'Well, silver linings and all that. Good, I'm glad to hear it. There's hope for Coco yet then,' she said.

'Can we open our presents yet?' Wilfred called from his place next to the tree.

'Soon, darling,' Florence said, turning to him. 'Won't be long now. Gosh, we're a much smaller party at Chalfield than we started with, aren't we? Araminta's told Rufus to stay at Steven's house for the time being. She said she needs time to think about their relationship. She understands why he is so angry about what Giles did, but seems rather disgusted by his behaviour yesterday, as am I, incidentally. Perhaps he'll take a leaf out of his wife's book and ease up on the drinking. If not, well, who knows what will happen between them...'

'Good for her,' Sister Veronica said. 'Show's she's got backbone. Some time apart will do them both good. So who's left in the house now?'

'Just you, me, Wilfred, Coco, Magnus, Cecily, Barnaby and Araminta. Oh, and Mrs Hardman – who is cooking up a mouthwatering Christmas lunch in the kitchen. Romilly went back home last night with her tail between her legs, and I have a feeling we won't be seeing so much of her from now on, which will do her children no end of good, give them a chance to start feeling much better about themselves, hopefully. Lucie caught an Uber home early this morning. She's much happier now, though, after what I explained to her.' Florence's eyes twinkled.

Sister Veronica shifted herself up a bit.

'What do you mean, what you explained to her?' she said.

'Well,' Florence said, a smile playing on her lips. 'I've decided to sell Chalfield Hall. It's the only way forward, and to be honest, as you know, I've never really liked the place anyway. It's a money pit, and has always felt soulless to me, and after everything that's happened this Christmas I wouldn't be happy here now anyway. Not with all these memories. Especially since I found out about Giles' embezzlement and his affair with Cecily. With the proceeds, I can pay off Giles' business debts, give all his workers their outstanding wages, and pay back Rufus' investment, and I'll have enough left over to buy any gorgeously pretty cottage of my choice, plus one for Magnus, Coco and Wilfred. And, of course, a large share will go to Ophelia and Sam, so they can start a fresh new life together.'

'Flo,' Sister Veronica said, smiling. 'What a marvellous idea.'

'And,' Florence said. 'I overheard Lucie talking to Neil on the phone about giving up her PhD, as they can't afford for her to do it. I think that's why she was so glum the other day, she must have been about to ask me for some money, then realised there wasn't any due to Giles' idiocy. Apparently, she was on the verge of resigning from it and going back to a nine-to-five paid job, just so they could keep the bailiffs from the door. So I've told her I'll lend her a generous amount, that she only needs to start paying back when they can afford to do so. She was absolutely over the moon, V. It was lovely to see her face light up.'

'How's Cecily taken the news?' Sister Veronica said, imagining the look on the woman's face when she realised she'd never be the dame of Chalfield Hall. She almost wished she'd been there to see it.

Florence laughed.

'Better than I expected,' she said. 'But she's not happy, started on the wine again, in fact, so goodness knows what she'll get up to later. I'd better put a lock on the wine cellar. Oh yes, and I'm going to donate a generous amount to you and your convent, V.'

Sister Veronica opened her mouth, a protest on the edge of her lips.

'No, don't say anything, V, I've made up my mind about it. You and the other sisters are free to use the money as you wish, donate it all to charitable causes if that's what you want, but I'm definitely giving it to you. Think of it as a final thank you for everything you've done this week.'

Sister Veronica smiled, and settled back into the large fluffy pillows Florence had positioned behind her back.

'Thank you, Flo,' she said quietly. 'You really don't have to, but I'm truly grateful for it.' Seeing Florence again, even under the most horrendous of circumstances, had unexpectedly warmed her heart and made it glow. She hadn't seen much of her family since entering the convent, none of the sisters did. Her dear parents were long buried, and were most likely having a wonderful time in heaven, hopefully sitting down to their celestial Christmas lunch right now. She felt closer to her cousin now than she ever had, and suspected they would remain that way for the rest of their lives. She, for one, would make a concerted effort to remain in touch with Flo, become better at writing letters and making phone calls. That was what Christmas was really about, she thought. Renewing that love between family members and friends. Of course, one could do that all year round, but the festive season offered an unprecedented opportunity for it, when most people had the time – if not always the inclination – to re-evaluate relationships.

The living-room door opened, and the serious face of Mrs Hardman appeared.

'Christmas lunch is nearly ready, Mrs Beresford,' she said quietly, before retreating. 'I'll be ready to serve up in five minutes.'

'Wonderful.' Florence slapped her hands on her knees and stood up. 'Oh, V, before I forget, a letter arrived for you yesterday, but I never had a chance to give it to you, what with all the horrendous goings-on.' She reached into the pocket of her trousers and withdrew a slightly crumpled envelope, passed it to her cousin, kissed her on the forehead, then exited the room with a smile.

Sister Veronica eyed the writing on the envelope with suspicion. She'd know that copperplate scrawl anywhere; it was Sister Julia Augusta's hand – her Mother Superior from the Convent of the Christian Heart. What on earth was she writing to her at Chalfield Hall for?

She tore open the envelope and withdrew the paper. A faint, familiar smell of incense wafted up from it.

Dear Sister Veronica, she read.

I hope you are having a restful, prayer-filled festive break. Sister Veronica snorted to herself.

I am writing to inform you that an emergency has occurred in one of our affiliated Christian Heart convents in Torquay, Devon. It is a place of convalescence, where people who have been injured in terrible accidents can come and stay and recuperate after they've been discharged from hospital. Many of the residents – nuns and patients alike – have been struck down by a virulent virus, and are now in South Devon Hospital. There are still a few patients remaining at the convent – who were lucky enough not to catch the virus – but who still require the care that the nuns were giving to them. One woman in particular, who is recovering from a car crash, requires immediate attention. However, the sister who was fulfilling that role is now very poorly herself and is unable to continue working. The convent's local bishop wrote to me asking if I had a robust, caring nun in my convent, who could be transferred to Torquay immediately after Christmas to continue caring for this woman. And, of course, I thought of you, Veronica. You are certainly robust, very caring in your own way, and more pointedly you seem to be allergic to staying at our convent in Soho for more than a few weeks at a time.

'Bah!' Sister Veronica said to the now empty living room. *Transfer me immediately?* she thought. *I don't think so, Mother Superior. I have too many things to do once I get back to London. I'm sure Sister Irene would be most willing to fulfil the role...*

Now before you challenge my words, the letter went on, almost as though Mother Superior had fortune-telling abilities, *I have given this matter a lot of thought and I'm afraid the decision to send you to Torquay is not up for discussion, Veronica. It is final. As you know, I have been extremely lenient on you over the last year, what with all your gallivanting and escapades, and you have just been lucky enough to spend Christmas away with family. So I know you will repay my kindness by not making a fuss about this, but by calmly packing your belongings on your return to the Convent of the*

Christian Heart, and willingly travelling to Torquay to care for this
poor woman who so badly needs your help. In fact, I have already
purchased a train ticket for you. One way, of course, as the role is
indefinite, and will last until the Sister who was the woman's previous
carer is fully better, has left hospital and has recuperated.

God bless and Merry Christmas,

Sister Julia Augusta

P.S. You may wish to research the distressing mental condition of
paranoia. I'm told the woman you will be looking after is suffering
from a hefty dose of this at the moment, due to the bad head injury
she suffered.

Sister Veronica slapped the letter down onto the duvet
covering her legs. So she was being sent away to Torquay, was
she? Without even being consulted about it? And what was all
this about paranoia? Goodness gracious, she'd never heard
anything like it. Well, she thought, the inklings of a new forthcoming adventure stirring in her stomach, cutting through her
initial indignation. At least her life could never be described as
boring. She swung her legs over the side of the sofa and gently
eased herself up. She sniffed the air, the rich scent of roast beef,
perfectly seasoned potatoes and a sensational-smelling stuffing
causing her to lick her lips. Fine, she decided. She would worry
about Torquay tomorrow. Right now, she had an enormous
Christmas lunch to eat. She plodded out towards the dining
room, breaking into a cheery hum, wondering if Wilfred the
walking encyclopaedia knew anything about paranoia...
perhaps, if she got the chance, she could question him about it
over pudding...

THE END

ACKNOWLEDGEMENTS

A huge thank you to Betsy, Fred and the whole team for their help in bringing this book out. Particularly to Ian Skewis, for being such a great editor to work with, Tara, for her fantastic organisation, Maria for all the publicity work, the ARC readers for taking the time to read and review The Tormented. And of course my wonderful family and friends, for just being there and eating copious amounts of chocolate with me.

A NOTE FROM THE PUBLISHER

Thank you for reading this book. If you enjoyed it please do consider leaving a review on Amazon to help others find it too.

We hate typos. All of our books have been rigorously edited and proofread, but sometimes mistakes do slip through. If you have spotted a typo, please do let us know and we can get it amended within hours.

info@bloodhoundbooks.com

Printed in Great Britain
by Amazon